TIME TRAVEL

Exploring Temporal Frontiers from Madman Mike to John Titor, Sergey Panamerenko, Kozyrev Mirrors, and the Timeless Montauk Project

Prabal Jain

Riverwood Capital

Copyright © 2023 Prabal Jain

All rights reserved

The characters and events portrayed in this book are fictitious. Any similarity to real persons, living or dead, is coincidental and not intended by the author.

No part of this book may be reproduced, or stored in a retrieval system, or transmitted in any form or by any means, electronic, mechanical, photocopying, recording, or otherwise, without express written permission of the publisher.

ISBN: 9798867926229

CONTENTS

Title Page
Copyright
Introduction
Part 1: The Time Machinist — 1
Introduction — 2
Chapter 1: Mike's Electrifying Experiment — 4
Chapter 2: Mike's Bold Move — 9
Chapter 3: Mike's Turning Point — 15
Chapter 4: The Power Behind the Plasma Tornado — 19
Chapter 5: The Leap into the Unknown — 23
Chapter 6: Exposing the Tale — 28
PART 2: Mirrors of Destiny: — 31
Introduction — 32
Chapter 1: Kozyrev Mirrors — 34
Chapter 2: The Torsion Mystery — 38
Chapter 4: Time's Dynamic Symphony — 42
Chapter 5: The Mirror's Embrace — 46
Chapter 6: Fear's Manifestation and Celestial Oddities — 53
Chapter 7: Embarking on the Ethereal Journey — 57
Chapter 8: Communing with The Observers — 60
Chapter 9: Unlocking Mysteries — 63

Part 3: Journey to Infinity	67
Introduction	68
Chapter 1: Decoding the Classified Gateway Report	70
Chapter 2: The Illusion of Reality	73
Chapter 3: Harmony of Hemispheres	76
Chapter 4: Clicking Out of Reality	82
Chapter 5: Harmonizing Frequencies	85
Chapter 6: The Click-Out Point	88
Chapter 7: Revealing the Missing Page and Gateway's Universal Purpose	92
Chapter 8: Navigating the Unknown	97
Part 4: Chronicles of Time	100
Introduction	101
Chapter 1: A Puzzling Admission	103
Chapter 2: From Fiction to Reality	106
Chapter 3: Exposing the Tale	111
Part 5: Savior of Tomorrow	116
Introduction	117
Chapter 1: A Glimpse Beyond	118
Chapter 2: The Time Traveler's Wisdom	121
Chapter 3: Revelations of Time Travel Technology	125
Chapter 4: The Practicalities of Time Travel	128
Chapter 5: The Legacy Unfolds	132
Chapter 6: Larry Haber's Role in the John Teeter Story	136
Chapter 7: John Teeter's Survival Advice and Personal Preparedness	139
Part 6: The Montauk Project	141
Introduction	142
Chapter 1: The Mysteries of Montauk	144

Chapter 2: Dual Realities Unveiled	147
Chapter 3: The Montauk Experiment	151
Chapter 4: Nightmares and Contingencies	155
Chapter 5: Shadows and Anomalies	159
Chapter 6: Exposing Credibility	163
Epilogue	167
About The Author	169
Books By This Author	171

INTRODUCTION

Embarking on a Chronological Odyssey

Welcome, dear reader, to a literary expedition that defies the confines of conventional storytelling—a journey that spans the epochs and explores the enigmatic realm of time travel. This book is not just a collection of chapters; it is a portal to temporal landscapes unbound by the constraints of reality.

Beyond the Ticking Clocks:

As you embark on this adventure, leave behind the ticking of mundane clocks and embrace the fluidity of time itself. The pages you hold in your hands are not mere parchment; they are gateways to eras past, present, and future. Prepare to witness the ebb and flow of history in ways you could never have imagined.

Temporal Portals and Parallel Realities:

The concept of time travel, an age-old fascination, takes center stage. Within these chapters, you will traverse temporal portals, stepping into parallel realities where the consequences of choices echo across the corridors of time. Brace yourself for a narrative that challenges your perception of cause and effect.

A Fusion of Science and Imagination:

Here, science and imagination dance in a delicate fusion. While the foundations are built on scientific theories and principles, the stories breathe with the creative energy of what-ifs and maybes. Quantum mechanics, temporal paradoxes, and the intricacies of the space-time continuum become companions on this literary odyssey.

Characters Across Centuries:

Meet characters who defy the linear progression of time—individuals whose destinies are interwoven with the fabric of temporal existence. Their journeys transcend centuries, posing questions about the fragility of our temporal reality and the profound impact of seemingly insignificant moments.

Temporal Ethics and Dilemmas:

As the narrative unfolds, so too do ethical dilemmas. What responsibility comes with the ability to manipulate time? Should the past be left untouched, or is it a canvas for revision? The exploration of these moral quandaries adds depth to the tapestry of temporal exploration.

The Timeless Allure:

This book invites you to succumb to the timeless allure of time travel—an allure that has captivated minds for generations. It is not just a literary endeavor but a philosophical inquiry into the nature of time, fate, and free will.

Beyond the Cover:

As you turn the first pages, remember that this is not merely a book; it is a vessel that transcends literary boundaries. What lies beyond the cover is an odyssey through the uncharted territories of the temporal unknown. So, fasten your seatbelt, dear reader, for the temporal adventure of a lifetime awaits. The journey begins now.

◆ ◆ ◆

PART 1: THE TIME MACHINIST

Madman Mike Markham's Journey through Temporal Frontiers

INTRODUCTION

Embarking on a Time-Defying Odyssey with Madman Mike Markham

In the realm of human inquiry, few quests captivate the imagination like the exploration of time. It's a journey that stretches the limits of our comprehension, challenging the very fabric of reality that envelops us. And in this enigmatic landscape of temporal exploration, Madman Mike Markham, a maverick treading the uncharted territories where time's secrets beckon.

Our narrative begins with a young visionary, a 21-year-old Mike Markham, who, fueled by insatiable curiosity, dared to construct a time machine. The porch of his modest abode transformed into a laboratory, he embarked on a journey that would transcend the ordinary and catapult him into the annals of the extraordinary.

In this introductory chapter, we delve into the genesis of Mike's odyssey, a tale that unfolds across three compelling interviews with the venerable Art Bell. From the inception of a humble prototype to the audacious act of liberating industrial-grade transformers, Mike's story is a tapestry woven with threads of innovation, controversy, and the relentless pursuit of the unknown. His experiments, culminating in a vortex that devoured objects and sent them to unknown destinations, opened a gateway to contemplation – a gateway that beckons us to question the very nature of our reality.

The tale of Madman Mike Markham invites us to join the odyssey, to question, to dream, and to explore the uncharted territories that await those who dare to defy the constraints of the present. As we turn the pages of this narrative, we are beckoned to peer into the unknown, where the very essence of existence is both the question and the answer. The adventure awaits – let us step into the vortex and embark on a time-defying odyssey with Madman Mike Markham.

◆ ◆ ◆

CHAPTER 1: MIKE'S ELECTRIFYING EXPERIMENT

Unleashing the Power

Mike, a curious inventor from Stanbury, Missouri, excitedly activated his invention, and suddenly, lasers sparked to life. The machine created an unexpected phenomenon—an 8-inch Vortex with ripples resembling those above a fire. Bewildered, Mike tossed a sheet metal screw into the mysterious field, and to his astonishment, it vanished.

In suspense, Mike powered down the machine, heading back to his house. Just as he thought he might have stumbled upon a teleportation breakthrough, he heard a clattering sound. The screw reappeared, rolling to a stop 2 feet from the box. Mike, the amateur inventor with a knack for electronics, pondered the implications. Little did he know, this experiment might have led to the invention of a time pillow. His backyard resembled an appliance graveyard, filled with dismantled TVs, radios, and CD players. Amidst the chaos of spools of copper wire and magnets, Mike embarked on his latest project—a modified Jacob's Ladder, producing climbing arcs of electricity.

JACOB'S LADDER

To achieve this electrifying spectacle, Mike needed a special transformer, not the Autobot kind, but an electronic one. Transformers, in this context, aren't robots from Cybertron but essential components for creating high-voltage power supplies. The need for a high voltage power supply in the tens of thousands of volts. The standard household voltage in the United States, at 120 or 240 volts, fell far short of his requirements. Undeterred, Mike, the transformer builder extraordinaire, set out to create his own.

He wound two separate coils of wire around a common core —one connected to the power source (the house's fuse box) and the other with varying turns to step up or step down the voltage. Engaging in a wire-coiling marathon, Mike lost count after about 400 turns. Nevertheless, he succeeded in stepping up his voltage from 120 to a whopping 20,000 volts. Now equipped with the necessary power supply for his climbing rods (or conductors), Mike revealed a quirky detail—he used wire hangers. A nod to those who understand the "no wire hangers ever" sentiment.

Now, here's the magic of the Jacob's Ladder in simple terms: The voltage applied to the conductors ionizes the air particles between the rods, allowing current to flow. The arc starts at the narrowest point where the rods are closest together, and the heat from the arc makes the surrounding air hotter and less dense.

However, Mike knew it wasn't foolproof. The arc needed initiation by manually adjusting the rods' distance. It was touchy, affected by air pressure, humidity, temperature changes, and even the presence of smoke or dust.

Enter Mike's ingenious idea: using lasers to heat the air around the conductors. This would lower air resistance, ionize it, and spark the arc to ignite on its own. Much to his disappointment, no spark ignited. However, as he was about to disconnect the machine, something strange caught his eye.

Hovering above the device was a sphere of distorted air, resembling the wavy mirage seen over a highway on a hot day. It wasn't a powerful ball of energy; rather, it was hardly visible unless you were actively looking for it. Uncertain about its nature or potential danger, Mike decided to conduct an experiment.

He tossed a sheet metal screw into the energy field, and to his amazement, the screw disappeared. Confused but intrigued, Mike patiently observed. After a moment, the screw fell out of the field and landed on the ground a couple of feet away. Intrigued by this unexpected phenomenon, he repeated the experiment, obtaining the same result each time.

The screw vanished momentarily upon entering the energy field, only to reappear a few seconds later. Mike found himself standing there, pondering whether his machine was teleporting objects or perhaps sending them a few seconds into the future.

Despite the machine eventually overloading, resulting in dead lasers and fried components, Mike remained convinced that he had stumbled upon something significant. Undeterred, he embarked on the next phase of his experiment. The burnt-out box of parts from his initial prototype served as the foundation for a new endeavor.

This time, Mike planned to scale up his invention significantly.

Instead of the modest 18-inch height of the prototype, he envisioned an 8-foot tall machine. To achieve this ambitious goal, he knew he needed access to much more power. With determination in his eyes, Mike Markham set out on the challenging task of rebuilding his time machine, ready to unravel the mysteries of time on a grander scale.

◆ ◆ ◆

CHAPTER 2: MIKE'S BOLD MOVE

Powering Up the Time Machine

Undeterred by setbacks, Mike was determined to scale up his time machine. While larger conductors and lasers were readily available, the real challenge lay in acquiring the power needed for his ambitious project.

His house provided a mere 120 volts, and although he successfully stepped it up to 20,000 volts for the prototype, his homemade transformer couldn't withstand the demands, giving out after just a few minutes. For the gander experiment, Mike needed transformers capable of handling 50,000 volts or more without breaking a sweat. These were not the kind of transformers one could find easily, and certainly not on a tight budget.

Undeterred by financial constraints, Mike hatched a plan—a risky one. Knowing of six industrial-grade transformers sitting idle in a yard, he called upon a couple of friends with pickup trucks. In broad daylight, they drove to the substation of the King City, Missouri power company, loaded up the transformers, and left. A few weeks later, the next version of Mike's machine was ready.

The new setup included transformers connected to the grid, upgraded lasers, and 4-foot-long 1-inch metal rods replacing the humble wire hangers. This transformed the machine into a formidable beast. The moment of truth arrived as Mike powered up the machine. A loud crack, a spark, and then darkness engulfed his house. The new machine had knocked out the power, not just in his house, but the entire town.

Undeterred by the mishap, Mike set to work. Through some tinkering, he managed to get the machine running without causing widespread blackouts. The machine, now a powerful entity, created an energy field or vortex a few feet wide. Excited and armed with lessons from previous tests, Mike sent various objects through the vortex, eager to unveil the capabilities of his revamped time machine.

From Experiment to Headlines

With the machine running smoothly and without causing townwide brownouts, Mike discovered a remarkable new development. The energy field or vortex created by the machine was now a few feet wide, but this time, objects sent through it weren't reappearing. They were vanishing, disappearing into the unknown.

On one fateful afternoon, Mike and his friends decided to push the boundaries. Curious if a larger object could traverse the vortex, they playfully shoved a couch into the energy field. To their amazement, the couch vanished. However, the good news was tinged with bad news—Mike's cat was on the couch at the time.

Now, in an empty living room, the group stood in awe, surrounded by the whirling field of energy. Suddenly, a pounding on the front door interrupted their shock. Opening the door, Mike faced eight deputies armed with a search warrant. His neighbors had reported strange activities, and the police quickly connected the dots between Mike's project and the missing equipment reported by the power company.

The experiment that was about to unveil new possibilities for time travel came to a screeching halt. Mike Markham found himself facing legal consequences—he was sentenced to 60 days in jail and placed on five years' probation for stealing transformers and power.

In jail, Mike's inventive mind didn't rest. He brainstormed ways to make the machine more efficient. However, the reality hit hard—he lost his house, his job, and became a pariah in his town due to the infamous brownouts caused by his experiments. It seemed like the end of Mike's time machine endeavors.

But then, an unexpected turn. Mike's story made the news, and the headlines read, "Kansas City Man Tries to Build Time Machine on Porch." A Missouri worker's attempt to create a time machine on his back porch became a sensational tale that captured the public's imagination, turning Mike Markham into an unwitting figure in the world of unconventional scientific pursuits. The news spread far and wide, capturing the attention of the public and even catching the eye of Art Bell, the renowned host of the Coast to Coast AM radio show.

The headline read, "Kansas City Man Tries to Build a Time Machine on Porch," highlighting Mike's unconventional project. While the contraption he devised wasn't dismissed entirely by scientists, it did raise eyebrows. The chairman of the physics department at the University of Missouri at Kansas City acknowledged that theoretical physicists were exploring similar concepts.

However, Mike's venture had unintended consequences. The Stanbery police reported that the voltage Markham diverted into his contraption caused power interruptions in and around the Northwest Missouri town of about 1,300 residents. Subsequently, Mike found himself facing legal trouble. He was arrested on January 29th on a felony charge of stealing transformers from a power generating station in King City. Pleading guilty, he was placed on five years' probation.

The transformers Mike took had a capacity of 12 to 76,000 volts each, posing risks of electrocution or explosion. Mike, who claimed to have two years of college-level electrical engineering, explained to the police that he was building a time machine but lacked sufficient power.

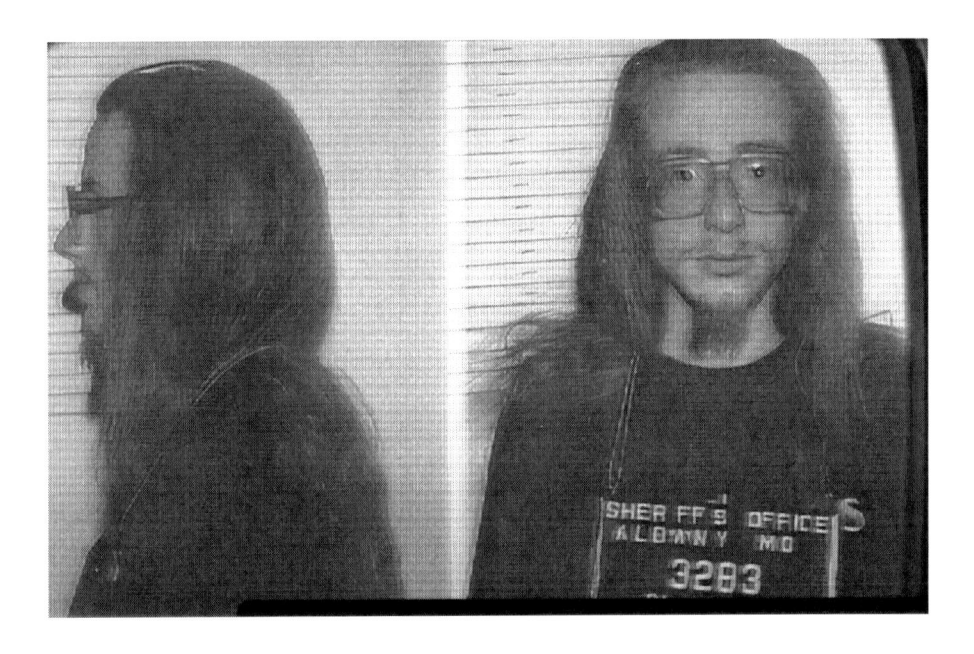

Enter Art Bell, a prominent figure in radio known for delving into unusual and unexplained phenomena. Bell took an interest in Mike's story and invited him for an hour and a half interview on the Coast to Coast radio show. During the interview, Mike came across as genuine, sharing his journey, challenges, and aspirations in the realm of time travel. This unexpected exposure on national radio not only amplified Mike's story but also changed the trajectory of his life in unforeseen ways.

◆ ◆ ◆

CHAPTER 3: MIKE'S TURNING POINT

From Radio Waves to a New Beginning

After Art Bell tracked down Mike Markham, the two engaged in a revealing interview on the Coast to Coast radio show. The hour-and-a-half conversation showcased not only Mike's legitimacy but also his considerable knowledge and expertise in electronics, a trait shared by the seasoned radio host, Art Bell.

Art delved into technical details with Mike, discussing the intricacies of transformers, turns, watts, amps, voltages, and the principles of stepping up and stepping down. Mike's understanding of these concepts demonstrated his genuine expertise. Art Bell, well-versed in electronics, knew that if Mike was faking it, he wouldn't be able to fool him.

Mike shared insights into his experiments, discussing the use of square waves for easy control of the duty cycle and voltage. Humble and unassuming, Mike wasn't seeking fame or attention. It was Art Bell who convinced him to share his story on air.

The interview resonated with millions of listeners, leading to an outpouring of support. Offers flooded in—people had transformers to donate, properties for him to use, and financial support to aid in building a new and larger machine. The possibility of mentorship and collaboration with those who believed in Mike's vision became a potential reality.

Art Bell asked Mike about the prospect of someone becoming his mentor and contributing funds for a grander version of the machine. Mike expressed enthusiasm, considering it a dream come true. In the following days, offers continued to pour in, and Mike, now supported by a team, formulated a plan.

Corresponding with physicists, Mike sought their insights on his technology and its potential applications for time travel. With guidance from scientists, he developed a concept involving rotating magnets to enhance control over the machine. Empowered by the newfound support, Mike secured a warehouse, gathered all necessary equipment, and gained access to additional resources for the next phase of his experimental journey.

Over the course of about a year, Mike diligently worked on building a newer, larger, and highly upgraded version of his time machine. This endeavor marked a significant milestone in his journey, culminating in the successful construction of a more advanced model.

The upgraded time machine proved its efficacy—it worked. Nearly 18 years after their initial conversation, Art Bell, the radio host, reconnected with Mike Markham. To Art's surprise, Mike was not only alive but thriving. Art had previously expressed concerns for Mike's safety, fearing he might have met a perilous fate during his ambitious experiments.

In their reunion, Art acknowledged his past apprehensions, humorously recalling calling Mike "madman" due to his worries about Mike potentially harming himself. Unlike some other individuals involved in time travel experiments whom Art had interviewed and subsequently lost contact with, Mike Markham had not only survived but also made substantial progress.

The catalyst for this transformation was Mike's previous appearance on Coast to Coast, which attracted benefactors, financial support, and equipment. This newfound support allowed Mike to set up a workspace in a warehouse in Overland Park, Kansas. There, he embarked on building several iterations of his time machine.

The most successful version utilized rotating magnets, a departure from the original small energy vortex. Mike referred to this innovative mechanism as a "plasma tornado." He explained the efficiency gains achieved by using the magnetic field to stir the plasma, creating a visually striking phenomenon.

◆ ◆ ◆

CHAPTER 4: THE POWER BEHIND THE PLASMA TORNADO

As Mike Markham delved into the intricacies of his upgraded time machine, he highlighted a key aspect—the immense power required to create what he termed a "plasma tornado." In simple terms, he explained the relationship between volts and the pressure driving electric current, drawing an analogy to water flow.

Recalling the evolution of his machines, Mike referenced his first prototype running at 20,000 volts. The next version, infamous for consuming a couch and a cat, operated at around 70,000 volts. The latest iteration in the warehouse, standing at about 15 feet tall, pushed the boundaries with a staggering 3 million volts.

Mike clarified the concept of volts as the pressure or force driving electric current. Drawing an analogy with a water hose, he compared amps to the amount of water flowing through the hose or the power running through a circuit. While households typically receive 100 to 200 amps of power, Mike's machine showcased that even with lower amps, extremely high voltage could be achieved through transformers.

To meet the power demands of his machine, Mike utilized electricity from the power company supplemented by a couple of generators. This ensured he had more than enough power to run his complex setup. The machine itself comprised two cylinders—one inside the other—with a circle of electromagnets creating a magnetic field around them. The result was a vortex of plasma inside, stirred by the rotating magnetic field.

In an intriguing connection, Art Bell brought up the Philadelphia Experiment, a mysterious event involving a naval experiment during World War II. Mike's description echoed similarities, involving high voltage and rotating magnetic fields. When Mike was initially arrested, he had candidly informed the police that he was building a time machine. Art Bell drew attention to the parallel electronic setups between Mike's project and the infamous Philadelphia Experiment, both involving the manipulation of high voltage and rotating magnetic fields.

Despite initial skepticism from law enforcement when Mike declared he was building a time machine upon his arrest, several scientists saw potential in his approach. They noted that if time travel were possible, Mike's technology seemed to align with the principles of Einstein's equations, which permit the concept of time travel.

Einstein's theories provided blueprints for various time travel designs, including the idea of gigantic spinning cylinders that could enable a traveler to circumnavigate the cylinder and return before their departure. Inspired by these theoretical possibilities, Mike delved into testing his machine's capabilities.

Initially, he sent small objects like bits of wood and baseballs through the vortex. These objects appeared to vanish initially, reminiscent of the earlier incident with the couch and the cat. However, instead of true disappearance, they reappeared in different locations, consistently ending up between 50 and 150 yards east or west of the machine. Mike hypothesized that this directional pattern might be influenced by Earth's rotation or magnetic field.

Despite the seeming incredibility of the story, Mike ensured that these tests were witnessed by a group of 15 people. Those who contributed money or equipment to the project were given the opportunity to be part of the experimental process. The tests were conducted with transparency, and the involvement of multiple witnesses added credibility to the ongoing experiments.

As the testing progressed, Mike introduced living subjects into the vortex—specifically, mice, hamsters, and guinea pigs, avoiding any repeats of the cat incident. Approximately 200 tests were conducted, involving both inanimate objects and animals. The results were consistent: objects and animals would momentarily vanish upon entering the vortex and reappear approximately two minutes later. Interestingly, the relocated objects and animals consistently ended up east or west of the machine, never north or south.

In a quest to understand the nuances of his machine's function, Mike varied the voltage and the speed of the magnets, discovering that these adjustments influenced the distance traveled by the objects during their temporal journey. The extensive and repetitive testing with a diverse range of subjects added a layer of credibility to Mike's ongoing exploration of the enigmatic realm of time travel.

PRABAL JAIN

❖ ❖ ❖

CHAPTER 5: THE LEAP INTO THE UNKNOWN

Mike's Astonishing Disappearance

After about 200 successful tests involving inanimate objects and animals, Mike Markham had honed the control over his time machine. Adjusting the voltage and magnet speed allowed him to predict where objects would end up and how long their disappearance would last. The experiments reached a critical point, leading to Mike contemplating the ultimate test.

In a moment of daring resolve, Mike stood in front of the vortex, took a deep breath, and jumped into the temporal void. There was a flash of light, and Mike vanished. Art Bell, who had closely followed the project and even planned a visit to the warehouse, found himself unable to locate Mike when he checked in. The media, including national coverage, reported that the "madman" was gone.

During this period of apparent disappearance, Mike experienced a disorienting journey. When he regained consciousness, he found himself lying in the middle of a field, far from the familiar confines of his warehouse. Struggling with the worst headache he had ever experienced, Mike faced a significant challenge—he had no memory of how he arrived there, not even recalling his own name.

Driven by instinct, Mike began walking, and over time, his memories gradually returned. Surprisingly, he discovered that he had traversed a considerable distance and ended up in Fairfield, Ohio, a suburb of Cincinnati—800 miles due east of the Overland Park warehouse. In a baffling twist, Mike realized he had jumped two years into the future.

Complicating matters, Mike lacked any form of identification, including a driver's license or credit cards. With no money to his name, he navigated to the nearest homeless shelter in search of sustenance and orientation. It was at the shelter that Mike encountered a newspaper, unraveling the startling truth of his temporal journey.

Having leaped into the future, Mike pieced together a new reality. Over the following years, he undertook odd jobs, scraped together enough funds, and eventually took a bus back to his warehouse in Overland Park. Mike Markham faced a disheartening reality upon returning to his Overland Park warehouse. The once bustling hub of temporal experimentation was now an empty space, devoid of the machine, videos documenting each test, and crucial notes and documentation. Whether it was the mysterious Men in Black or a mundane landlord disposing of perceived abandoned property, the result was the same—everything was gone.

The loss was profound, erasing not only the tangible equipment worth millions but also wiping out Mike's invaluable records. Memory gaps added to the challenge, leaving him unable to recall donors and supporters whose names were crucial for his project. Despite this setback, Mike believed he could reconstruct the machine, estimating he retained 90 to 95% of the necessary information. However, the endeavor would demand significant financial investment.

In his third appearance on Coast to Coast, Mike recounted his tumultuous journey to Art Bell, who, along with the audience, eagerly sought updates on "madman" Markham. Despite not actively seeking financial aid, Mike found himself once again surrounded by people willing to assist. Suggestions poured in, including setting up a GoFundMe account for crowdfunding and exploring a potential book deal. While Mike acknowledged his lack of authorial skills, the idea of collaborating with a ghostwriter to convey the technical details intrigued him.

Another intriguing proposition surfaced—collaboration with the government, specifically mentioning DARPA (Defense Advanced Research Projects Agency). Art Bell, foreseeing potential challenges, cautioned Mike about potential strings attached to such partnerships, emphasizing the importance of careful consideration.

As Mike navigated these options, Art Bell encouraged him to persevere in his pursuits. The update on "madman" Markham left the audience wondering about the future, eager to witness the next chapter in Mike's relentless quest for understanding and harnessing the mysteries of time travel.

Into the Unknown

Mike Markham, undeterred by setbacks, continued his research and experiments under the encouragement of Art Bell. The world eagerly awaited updates on the endeavors of "madman" Markham, and during his appearances, he shared his aspirations for the future. Mike aimed to enhance his ability to travel through time, addressing challenges that surfaced in his experiments.

A significant obstacle in Mike's path was the unpredictable behavior of metal when passing through the temporal vortex. Metal items would sometimes reappear intact, while in other instances, they exploded into showers of sparks. Through trial and error, Mike discovered that constructing a metal tube in a specific way could turn it into a Faraday cage. This ingenious solution allowed the tube to traverse the portal unharmed, with anything inside, including metal objects, remaining unaffected.

Continuing his documentation and experiments, Mike built a substantial online following. In a notable post, he announced his readiness to embark on another journey, this time within the safety of the metal tube. The plan was to take essential items, such as his cell phone, ensuring he had the necessary tools, notes, photographs, and even money on the other side.

The last communication from Mike indicated his intention to venture through time inside the protective tube. However, after this announcement, silence enveloped his whereabouts. Art Bell, always vigilant, continued to monitor Mike's activities. It wasn't until a disturbing call during one of Art's radio shows that a potential clue emerged.

The caller presented a newspaper article from 1930 describing the discovery of a drowned man whose body washed up on the beach. The intriguing aspect was that the man was found inside a peculiar metal drum. The article noted the discovery of a small rectangular device on the man, which defied explanation. With no identification on the man, the mystery deepened, leaving everyone to wonder if this was a glimpse into the fate of Mike Markham.

The journey of "madman" Markham remained shrouded in uncertainty, with his fate and destination unknown. Only time would reveal the next chapter in this extraordinary tale of temporal exploration.

◆ ◆ ◆

CHAPTER 6: EXPOSING THE TALE

Madman Mike Markham's Time Travel Odyssey

In the realm of beloved episodes on Art Bell's show, Mike's story holds a special place among fans. Art, renowned for his storytelling prowess, skillfully navigates through the intricacies of Mike's journey. From the early days of building a Jacob's Ladder on his porch to the transformative events in the warehouse, including the 2-year time jump, Art weaves the narrative with a perfect pace, keeping listeners captivated.

Reflecting on the saga of madman Mike Markham, renowned as one of the best time travel stories, a lingering question arises: Is it true? The answer to this inquiry remains veiled in uncertainty, leaving room for speculation and contemplation. As enthusiasts and skeptics alike ponder the validity of Mike's time travel odyssey, the tale continues to captivate the imagination, transcending the boundaries of reality and fiction.

Separating Fact from Fiction

As we delve deeper into the chronicles of Madman Mike Markham, it becomes apparent that the internet is rife with misinformation about his journey. In his final interview with Art Bell, Mike dispels some of these myths, clarifying that he never sent a cat through the portal and addressing the fabricated tale of a man washing ashore in a metal drum in 1930.

Contrary to recent rumors suggesting Mike's demise, he is still very much alive, though his life has been spent largely in the realm of technology. The enduring question persists: What about the machine? When Mike, at the tender age of 21, crafted the prototype on his porch, his profound knowledge of electrical engineering left a lasting impression. While scientists were skeptical about the feasibility of a time machine, they acknowledged that, theoretically, such a device would involve high voltage and magnetism.

The convergence of Tesla's musings on electromagnetism and Einstein's revelation that gravity could enable time travel laid the theoretical groundwork. Mike Markham's endeavor hinted at harnessing electromagnetism to create a vortex with exceedingly high gravity. This concept, while speculative, aligns with the scientific understanding that gravity can dilate time. Mike asserted that his electromagnetism, 10 to the 30th times stronger, could achieve this without the need for a black hole.

As Art Bell's audience chimed in with questions and critiques, Mike demonstrated readiness to address them. He delved into a common gripe with time travel stories, highlighting the inconsistency in scenarios where a time machine could move someone precisely into the future. Mike questioned the narrative coherence in such instances, emphasizing the need for logical consistency in exploring the intricacies of time travel.

Navigating the Spacetime Conundrum

In the labyrinth of time travel tales, a glaring inconsistency often overlooked is the neglect of spatial considerations. Imagine a time machine propelling you ten minutes into the future. While time is traversed, space is not, and this poses a profound quandary. Earth hurtles through space at breakneck speeds: spinning at 1,000 mph, orbiting the sun at 66,000 mph, our solar system whizzing through the galaxy at 500,000 mph, and the galaxy itself hurtling at 1.3 million miles per hour. In ten minutes, your stationary position will have covered almost 990,000 miles in space. Yet, time machine stories seldom grapple with this spatial dilemma; Earth remains steadfast in its cosmic dance.

However, Madman Mike Markham offers a unique perspective. He contends that his time machine remains synchronized with the gravitational center of the Earth. In doing so, he not only transcends temporal boundaries but also navigates the vast cosmic expanse, addressing the often-overlooked spatial aspect inherent in time travel.

The trilogy of interviews, meticulously linked below, unveils Mike Markham's narrative. Calm and humble, he fields questions without an overt agenda to prove himself. Notably, it was not Mike who sought the spotlight but Art Bell who, compelled by the enigma, pursued him.

While skepticism may shroud Mike Markham's time travel odyssey, the fact remains—he is here. The lingering question persists: If one has indeed unlocked the secret to time travel, why remain in the present? As eyes may roll and judgments may be passed, Mike's story stands as a testament to the audacious dreamers who challenge the bounds of conventional thinking. In a world where temporal manipulation might one day become reality, pioneers like Mike Markham could hold the key to unlocking the mysteries of time.

◆ ◆ ◆

PART 2: MIRRORS OF DESTINY:

A Voyage into the Secrets of Kozyrev Mirrors and the Essence of Time

INTRODUCTION

In the frigid embrace of a remote village above the Arctic Circle, December 1990 witnessed the inception of an audacious scientific venture. Two Russian scientists embarked on a quest that defied the boundaries of human understanding. Their mission: to unlock the latent powers of human perception, delving into the realms of enhanced ESP (Extrasensory Perception).

The nucleus of their endeavor was a peculiar device, a large tube crafted from rolled aluminum, concealing within it a solitary chair. Yet, as the apparatus took form, an eerie aura enveloped the village. Unexplained phenomena danced in the frigid air—disc-shaped lights circled the laboratory, ethereal balls of energy materialized and dissipated, and even the Northern Lights, a celestial spectacle, assumed an unusually vivid and tangible form.

Amidst this spectral ballet, an unshakable sense of foreboding emanated from the laboratory. The device, designed to shield subjects from electromagnetic interference and amplify their inherent biological energy, held a promise yet unrevealed.

The endeavor faced considerable reluctance, but when the first brave soul occupied the chair, an eruption of energy transfixed the observers. The device had functioned, but the consequences surpassed expectations. Beyond augmenting psychic capabilities, it unfurled an unexpected gateway—subjects could now peer into any place across the globe and traverse the tapestry of time itself.

These groundbreaking experiments substantiated a theory proposed in the 1950s: the construct of time, as conventionally understood, was an illusion. The narrative unfolds, beckoning the reader into a world where reality blurs, and the boundaries between perception and actuality dissolve.

❖ ❖ ❖

CHAPTER 1: KOZYREV MIRRORS

In a small, remote village above the Arctic Circle, an unusual experiment unfolded in 1990, orchestrated by two Russian scientists, Dr. Trevumov and Dr. Kaznachive. Their focus was the exploration of heightened human perception through the utilization of a peculiar apparatus—an aluminum chamber adorned with a curved wall, concealing a chair within.

A volunteer, entrusted with the task, stood within the confines of this aluminum sanctum. His mission: to gaze upon the curved wall, conjuring mental images of ancient symbols studied prior to his entry. As he endeavored to immerse himself in the experiment, the narrative took a brief detour, attempting to create a mental tableau, a theater of the mind.

However, the attempt at theatricality was met with interruption, prompting a transition to straightforward narration. The volunteer, ensconced within the aluminum chamber, grappled with an unsettling progression of sensations. A primordial fear, instinctual and deep-rooted, enveloped him, urging an immediate departure from the contraption.

Dr. Trevumov and Dr. Kaznachive, overseeing the experiment, reassured the volunteer, attributing his unease to a common reaction. Persistence, they insisted, would lead to an eventual alleviation of discomfort. Similar experiences were shared by volunteers in multiple study sites across Russia.

With the passage of time, the volunteer's nausea waned, replaced by a disorienting sensation akin to floating. The overwhelming fear metamorphosed into a profound calmness. Mirroring his reflection in the curved wall began to lose definition, revealing its translucency. Through the semi-transparent barrier, an unexpected vista unfolded.

The aluminum chamber, nestled within a small concrete lab, was ostensibly in the Arctic Circle. Yet, the volunteer's gaze transcended the aluminum confines, presenting a sunny day with sounds of birdsong and children's laughter. As relaxation set in, the vision intensified, blurring the lines between reality and a seemingly impossible experience.

Effortlessly, the volunteer traversed the chamber wall, seamlessly entering the vivid panorama. The surreal encounter felt palpably real, defying the logical confines of the Arctic laboratory. As the man surrendered to the ethereal pull of the aluminum chamber, the transition into an alternate reality was seamless. The once-impenetrable barrier dissolved effortlessly, granting him entry into a vivid realm that defied the boundaries of possibility. The sensation was tangible, an undeniable reality, even though logic screamed that it couldn't be.

Floating in this extraordinary dimension, the man found himself trailing a child of about five or six years. Drawn closer, he discerned the boy walking along a sidewalk in an unidentified location. Perplexingly, the man's attempts to survey his surroundings proved futile, as if the periphery of his vision was smeared.

Yet, the boy remained in sharp focus. Nostalgia enveloped the man as he recognized the familiar shoes and clothes of his own childhood. A surge of electricity coursed down his spine when the boy turned around, revealing a younger version of himself.

Gradually, the surroundings came into sharper relief. The man realized he stood just blocks away from his childhood home. The distant hum of traffic, originating from a busy intersection half a mile away, and the laughter of playing children in a nearby park, became audible. The small aluminum chamber, though fading, still retained an elusive connection.

In a surreal twist, the man found himself caught in a moment 30 years in the past. The boy, seemingly aware, posed a question that defied temporal logic: "Who are you?" In an instant, the portal to the past closed, snapping the man back to the present day. The vision ended, leaving behind a profound contemplation of an inexplicable connection across time.

This mesmerizing experience, among dozens meticulously documented, unfolds within the annals of a study that delves into realms where science meets the supernatural. The man's journey into his own past is but a glimpse into the extraordinary occurrences witnessed within the confines of the aluminum chamber.

Nikolai Kozyrev, a Russian physicist whose pioneering work in astrophysics sparked both innovation and controversy in the early 20th century. As the stage is set for the scientific discourse that follows, the reader is primed for a journey into the uncharted territories where Kozyrev's theories continue to stir debate and intrigue.

❖ ❖ ❖

CHAPTER 2: THE TORSION MYSTERY

While Nikolai Kozyrev may not have achieved household name status, his influence on the scientific landscape of the early 20th century was undeniable. A Russian physicist of both innovation and controversy, Kozyrev's theories continue to spark debates, their relevance echoing through time.

In the tumultuous realm of astrophysics, Kozyrev's pioneering spirit led to discoveries that initially faced rejection but eventually stood the test of validation. In 1958, his assertion of volcanic activity on the moon was met with skepticism from the scientific community. The dismissal, however, would be short-lived as subsequent Apollo lunar missions unveiled the lunar landscape, aligning with Kozyrev's earlier claims. The moon's volcanic reality, once doubted, emerged from the shadows of skepticism into the light of undeniable truth.

Kozyrev's intellectual pursuits extended to the study of variable stars — celestial entities that undergo fluctuations in brightness. Amidst controversy, he introduced the concept of torsion fields, a notion that would become central to his body of work. Torsion, in its simplest manifestation, involves the twisting of an object in response to applied torque — a familiar action, akin to wringing out a wet cloth.

Yet, in the realm of theoretical physics, torsion takes on a profound dimension. It represents the twisting of space-time itself, a departure from the conventional narrative of Einstein's theory of relativity. While Einstein's theory depicts gravity as the warping or curving of space and time in the presence of mass and energy, Kozyrev's addition of torsion introduces a novel perspective.

In the familiar analogy of the rubber sheet, a staple in explaining general relativity, the addition of torsion transforms the narrative. Imagine not just a dip or curve in the sheet caused by a massive object like a planet, but a complete twist or torsion. Holding one end of a slinky exemplifies this, where torsion manifests as the twisting of space-time.

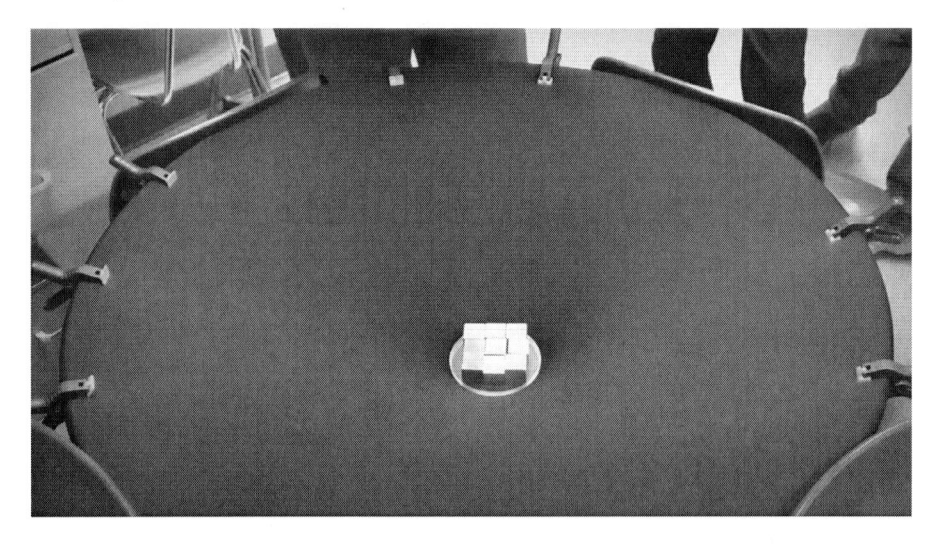

Torsion, a cornerstone of Kozyrev's enigmatic theories, holds the potential to unravel mysteries that extend beyond the confines of conventional understanding.

Beyond the Twists of Time

As we delve deeper into the complexities of torsion, envision holding one end of a slinky. Feel the wind whispering through the coils, creating a melodious symphony. A spring, a simple yet marvelous creation, captivating the imagination of both young and old alike. The slinky dance is a universal delight, a source of joy for boys and girls alike.

Extend the analogy further – imagine pulling the ends of the slinky. It doesn't just bend; it twists in a manner reminiscent of the twists embedded in Einstein's cartoon theory. This theory, unlike the straightforward curvature caused by mass and energy, proposes an additional element – the twist. This twist, according to Einstein, originates from the spinning of subatomic particles. However, Kozyrev, a dissenter in the scientific choir, introduces a different perspective.

Contrary to mainstream science asserting the emptiness of space, Kozyrev contends that there exists an invisible medium saturating the cosmos – The Ether. While The Ether's presence has ancient roots, it fell out of favor in the 19th century due to experiments seemingly unable to detect it. But Kozyrev challenges this dismissal, drawing parallels with the environments essential for the flight of birds or the swim of fish. Just because it eluded detection doesn't negate its existence.

Consider the journey of light, traversing vast distances from distant stars to our eyes. Mainstream science claims it moves through nothing, but Kozyrev insists this is implausible. The medium through which light moves, according to him, is The Ether – a dynamic, interactive force, not a static bystander. It's a medium alive with energy, akin to the lively interactions between fish and water or birds and air.

For Kozyrev, time is not a passive dimension; it possesses both energy and structure. Time, he argues, flows through and interacts with The Ether, creating ripples or waves of torsion. It's a bold assertion – time, not just a measure, but a physical force actively shaping the universe's existence. In Kozyrev's narrative, time becomes the heartbeat of the cosmos, orchestrating the symphony of existence itself.

❖ ❖ ❖

CHAPTER 4: TIME'S DYNAMIC SYMPHONY

A River Beyond Perception

In the mesmerizing realm of Kozyrev's theories, time emerges as more than a mere observer of the universe – it becomes an active participant, a force intricately woven into the fabric of existence. According to Kozyrev, time is the heartbeat of the universe, pulsating with energy that resonates through matter and space.

This pulsating energy isn't uniform; rather, it exhibits diverse densities. Time, as Kozyrev envisions it, can move at varying speeds, it can be accelerated, decelerated, and astonishingly, it can even move in reverse. The river of time, a metaphor we commonly associate with the unidirectional flow of past to present to future, takes on a dynamic form in Kozyrev's paradigm.

Much like a river shaping the landscapes it flows through, time energy influences everything it encounters. It impacts physical matter, including Earth and its inhabitants. It plays a role in the cosmic dance of galaxies, determines the orbits of planets, and breathes life into the shining stars scattered across the vast expanse of the universe.

The influence of time energy extends to the microcosm of our daily lives. It affects the weather, guides the growth of plants, and even intricately shapes the unique features encoded in our

DNA, such as the color of our eyes. The analogy of the river extends further – just as one can paddle a raft to alter its speed or direction, Kozyrev suggests that our perception of time is akin to floating on the river's surface.

In this dynamic model, we are carried along by the current of time, but with intentional effort, we can influence its flow. We can accelerate, decelerate, or even reverse our temporal journey, mirroring the varied actions one can take on a river. The past, the present, and the future, Kozyrev contends, coexist simultaneously, much like the river that remains behind us and stretches ahead.

The Mirror's Dance: Bending the Threads of Time

Kozyrev's groundbreaking experiments catapult us into the profound realization that time, far from a linear procession, is a simultaneous and infinite entity. His meticulous studies, utilizing pendulums and gyroscopes to unveil the elusive torsion fields and time energy, stand as a testament to the malleability of temporal dimensions.

In one captivating experiment, Kozyrev fixed his gaze on a distant star, recognizing that the light reaching us is a relic of its past. Astonishingly, he detected torsion from this celestial beacon, affirming that the influence of time is not confined by the speed of light. But Kozyrev's exploration did not halt at the past; he ventured into the present and future coordinates of this cosmic luminary, uncovering a fascinating revelation. Torsion, he found, was not only real but operated at speeds surpassing the swiftness of light – an instantaneous force transcending temporal constraints.

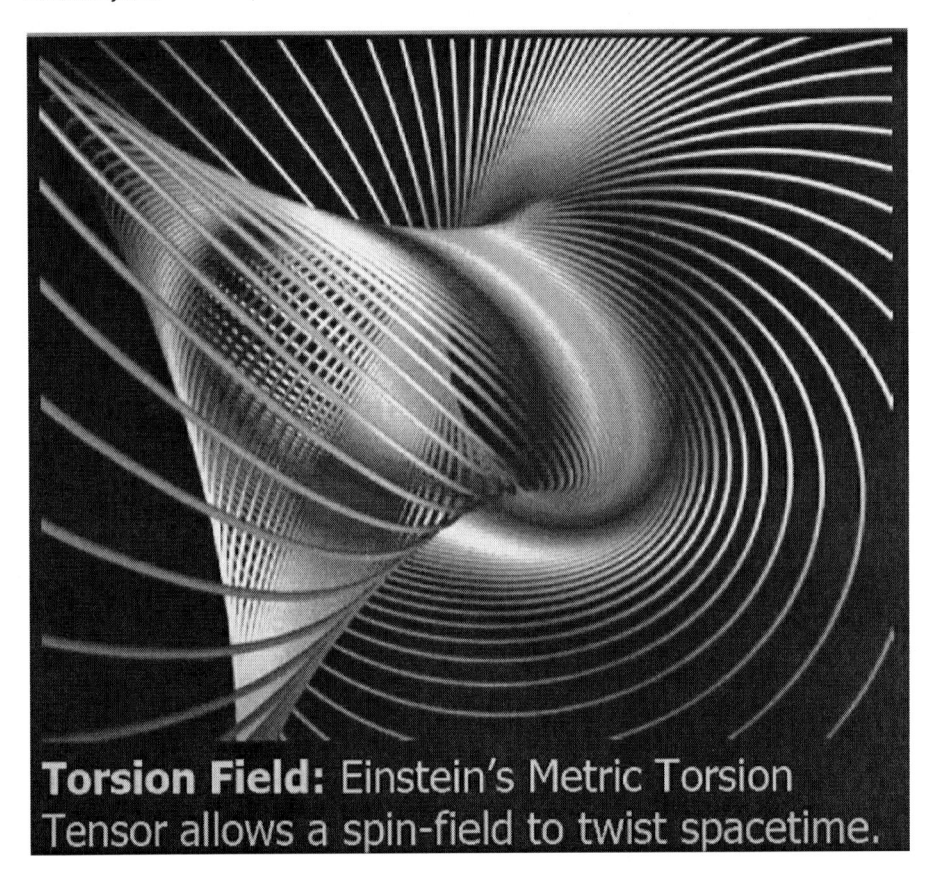

Torsion Field: Einstein's Metric Torsion Tensor allows a spin-field to twist spacetime.

Kozyrev's audacious assertion echoed through the corridors of scientific understanding. According to him, the traditional notions of past and future are mere metaphors, and in reality, there is only an eternal now. He proposed a symbiotic relationship between time and human consciousness, suggesting that concepts like intuition and foresight are manifestations of our minds tapping into the vast reservoir of time energy.

In a profound leap, Kozyrev theorized that human consciousness could, in turn, influence time. Thoughts and emotions, as carriers of energy, possess the ability to shape the physical world, creating a dynamic interplay with the temporal fabric. As time is not a passive dimension but an active force susceptible to concentration and redirection, Kozyrev's insights challenge conventional boundaries.

The climax of Kozyrev's revelations takes us to the heart of time travel. He proposed the creation of a mirror with the extraordinary capability to bend anything, including time itself. The construction of a machine to substantiate this theory marked a pivotal moment in the exploration of temporal frontiers. Kozyrev envisioned a future where mirrors become portals, enabling humanity to traverse the intricate tapestry of time.

◆ ◆ ◆

CHAPTER 5: THE MIRROR'S EMBRACE

Exposing the Secrets of Time

Kozyrev's audacious claim that a mirror could bend the fabric of reality itself, including time, propelled him into the realm of experimentation. To substantiate his groundbreaking theory, he ventured into the construction of a machine, envisioning the transformative potential of mirrors in reshaping our understanding of time travel.

Drawing inspiration from the historical use of concave mirrors, Kozyrev delved into their ability to concentrate light. The ancient Greeks and Romans, well-acquainted with these mirrors, harnessed their power to focus sunlight, igniting ceremonial torches and even kindling sacrificial fires. Mirrors became instruments of warfare, reflecting sunlight onto enemy ships to set them ablaze.

Throughout the medieval and Renaissance eras, concave mirrors became indispensable tools for scientists and alchemists exploring the mysteries of optics and light. Isaac Newton himself utilized concave mirrors to concentrate light in his telescopes. In the contemporary landscape, these mirrors find ubiquitous application in optical equipment, projectors, headlights, and communication devices, showcasing their versatility.

Kozyrev, recognizing the potential of mirrors to redirect energy, embarked on a journey that extended beyond the visible spectrum. He believed that a mirror, particularly a concave one, could bend not only light but also microwaves, lasers, ultraviolet rays, and even particles from space. His invention, a meticulously crafted thin sheet of metal bent into a spiral using Fibonacci-based geometry, emerged as a novel device capable of focusing time energy.

In the early stages of experimentation, Kozyrev, with an inclination towards aluminum, discovered that time energy responded most effectively to this metal. His initial prototype, operating at the microscopic level, purportedly enabled him to glimpse ten seconds into the future.

As Kozyrev's groundbreaking research delved into the realm of time manipulation, the Soviet government, recognizing the gravity of his discoveries, swiftly classified his work as a state secret. Undeterred by the shroud of secrecy, Kozyrev set his sights on a new frontier—a larger experiment encapsulated within a special mirrored chamber. The interior walls, entirely cloaked in the mystical properties of his special mirror, held the promise of accelerating time within the capsule.

The concept of manipulating time using mirrors echoed through history, resonating with the intuitive musings of other visionaries. Nostradamus, with his metal egg and a concave mirror, gazed into the future to craft his enigmatic predictions. Leonardo da Vinci, in one of his notebooks, envisioned a mirror chamber—a room enveloped by mirrored walls.

As Kozyrev delved into this new prototype, the watchful eyes of the Soviet government intensified their scrutiny. Simultaneously, the CIA, always attuned to the forefront of scientific exploration, couldn't overlook the implications of Kozyrev's work. The convergence of scientific intrigue and geopolitical tension heightened the stakes.

However, fate took an unexpected turn. On February 27, 1983, just as Kozyrev stood on the precipice of testing his revolutionary machine, he succumbed to a sudden and mysterious death, attributed to kidney failure. The circumstances surrounding his demise only added to the shadows encircling his research.

The veil of secrecy extended beyond borders, with American and Soviet intelligence both delving into the realm of psychic phenomena. Project Stargate, a well-known American program, explored various psychic abilities, focusing particularly on remote viewing. On the Soviet side, declassified CIA documents reveal their deep involvement in parapsychology and psychic espionage, with seemingly greater success in their endeavors.

As the calendar flipped to December 1990, The Institute of Experimental Medicine of the Academy of Sciences Siberian Branch became the stage for an audacious experiment. The centerpiece of this venture was the enigmatic Causal Mirror, a testament to Kozyrev's pioneering research, meticulously assembled in the northernmost settlement of Asia, Dixon.

The Causal Mirror, a spiral-shaped metal structure the size of a small closet, harbored the ambition to capture and focus psychic energy. However, from the moment of its activation, the facility and the town of Dixon became entwined in a tapestry of peculiar occurrences, chronicled in the book "Cosmic Consciousness of Humanity" by Drs. Kaznachive and Travamov. This literary account, easily accessible through the provided link, unfolds the intriguing events that unfolded during the study, complete with interviews, transcripts, and illustrations.

The initiation of the mirror brought forth an unexpected phenomenon—an intense field of fear enveloped the vicinity. Testimonies from researchers vividly describe an overwhelming sense of dread, akin to a wild terror, tangible and inexplicable. This fear manifested as a substantial force, almost palpable, inducing physical reactions in those present.

December 24th, 1990, marked a turning point. As researchers entered the room, an emotional pressure, laden with an eerie fear, gripped the atmosphere. Despite attempts to dismiss it, the researchers found it challenging to linger around the mirrors. The fear, described as a substance emanating from the Kozyrev space, permeated the room, leaving an indelible mark on the participants.

Test subjects shared their unsettling experiences. Some felt an unpleasant cold, dizziness, trembling hands, and a heavy head. The very air in the room seemed to undergo a transformation. The fear, an entity in itself, emanated from the mirror, establishing a formidable presence that initially deterred anyone from approaching it.

PRABAL JAIN

◆ ◆ ◆

CHAPTER 6: FEAR'S MANIFESTATION AND CELESTIAL ODDITIES

As the experiment unfurled, the pervasive fear emanating from the Kozyrev space became a palpable substance, enveloping the room. Its potency was such that, at the experiment's outset, an unspoken consensus emerged—nobody dared to approach the mirror. Opening the door felt akin to plunging into icy waters, inducing shivers and a reluctance to draw near. The fear intensified, teetering on the brink of compelling a hasty retreat.

Simultaneously, powerful bursts of energy, dubbed "plasmoids" by the researchers, materialized above the device. These ethereal phenomena bore a striking resemblance to ball lightning, evoking an otherworldly ambiance. Beyond the laboratory's confines, denizens of the town and lab employees reported witnessing enigmatic objects in the sky, adding a layer of mystique to the unfolding narrative.

Accounts of red glimmering circles, UFOs resembling ellipses radiating red and white light, and beams of light sweeping the heavens painted a surreal tableau. Witnesses recounted these celestial apparitions with a mix of awe and trepidation, amplifying the enigmatic atmosphere surrounding the experiment.

As the clock ticked, individuals summoned the courage to step into the Kozyrev mirror, propelling the narrative into a realm of even greater peculiarity.

The Kozyrev Mirror's Pioneering Experiment

Here unfolds the crux of the experiment—an operator nestled within a Causal Mirror in Dixon, while another person occupies a mirror in the distant town of Novosibirsk, separated by a staggering 1400 miles. The operator's task was to concentrate on a symbol and transmit it psychically to the receiver in Novosibirsk. The results, when unveiled, proved to be nothing short of astonishing.

On days when the Earth's magnetosphere rested in tranquility, the success rate oscillated between zero and ten percent. Yet, when the magnetosphere stirred during solar storms, a surge in activity was noted. The correlation between the Earth's magnetic fluctuations and the experiment's efficacy raised intriguing questions about the interplay between psychic phenomena and cosmic forces.

The exploration of the Kozyrev mirror had just scratched the surface. With each symbolic transmission and celestial enigma, the narrative burgeoned, beckoning participants and readers alike into a realm where the boundaries between fear, psychic energies, and the cosmos blurred into an intricate tapestry of the unknown.

As the experiment delved deeper, the surprising correlation between Earth's magnetospheric activity and the success rate of symbolic transmissions unfolded. On days of magnetic serenity, the success rate lingered between zero and ten percent. However, during the crescendo of solar storms, the receiver adeptly captured the operator's transmitted image, showcasing a success rate ranging from 30 to 45 percent. A peculiar tether between human consciousness and the Earth's magnetic field seemed to emerge, echoing Nikolai Kosarev's foundational theory linking solar weather, torsion waves, and their pervasive impact.

Building upon this intriguing revelation, a subsequent experiment involved two operators stationed in distinct Kozyrev mirrors across different cities. Their focus shifted to projecting images into the Earth's magnetosphere. The ripple effect resonated globally as 5,000 participants spanning 12 countries endeavored to attune to this energy and decipher the transmitted symbols. Astonishingly, when the magnetosphere danced with solar energy, the success rate soared to an unprecedented 95 percent.

This revelation not only astonished the overseeing scientists but also piqued the interest of the CIA, an avid observer of these unfolding phenomena. Notably, children, particularly those from spiritual and shamanic backgrounds, exhibited an uncanny prowess in these psychic endeavors.

In a test where the mirror operator merely conceived a number instead of an image, these intuitive young minds accurately received the numerical information, translating it into vivid drawings. Symbol 63 materialized in their illustrations, followed by Symbol 32, unraveling a tapestry of interconnected consciousness and cosmic resonance.

As volunteers acclimated to the Kozyrev mirror's embrace, extending their stays to seven hours or more, the metamorphosis within became apparent. Initially fraught with bodily tremors and enveloped in pressure, participants transcended into an ethereal lightness, akin to a departure from their corporeal selves. The Kozyrev space, once met with trepidation, evolved into a realm where the boundaries of self and cosmos blurred, fostering an immersive journey into the

PRABAL JAIN

unknown.

❖ ❖ ❖

CHAPTER 7: EMBARKING ON THE ETHEREAL JOURNEY

Navigating Kozyrev Space

Within the Kozyrev space, a transformative odyssey unfolded, marked by shared sensations and visions among participants. The initial tremors and heady pressure gave way to an otherworldly lightness, akin to a departure from the confines of the self. Coined as "Kozyrev space," this ethereal realm became a collective tapestry of experiences, forging a shared consciousness among those who ventured within.

As if guided by a cosmic choreography, individuals reported synchronous encounters within Kozyrev space. The overwhelming sense of weightlessness and a feeling of soaring through space enveloped nearly 90 percent of participants. Faces flickering before their eyes, black clouds resembling a descent into a cosmic abyss – these were not isolated occurrences but shared threads woven into the fabric of Kozyrev space.

A captivating chart within the book authored by Travumov and Kaznachieve cataloged these common experiences. Amid longer sessions, a peculiar yet recurring phenomenon emerged – the visualization and manifestation of symbols. Hovering in the air, these symbols, described as swirling and radiant, materialized in the room, each emitting an eerie neon glow. Astonishingly, these symbols weren't confined to individual minds; they transcended mental landscapes to manifest collectively in the physical space.

This cosmic lexicon extended beyond the realms of personal imagination, revealing a repository of two thousand distinct symbols. A linguist delving into this ethereal language found that 80 percent traced their origins to ancient cultures, with a pronounced resonance with ancient Sumerian symbolism. The convergence of symbols, witnessed independently by isolated individuals, attested to a shared consciousness traversing the boundaries of space and time.

As participants emerged from the transcendent Kozyrev space, an array of transformations awaited them. Minds seemed to operate with newfound swiftness, reflected in elevated IQ scores, expanded memory capacities, and a surge in creativity. Astonishingly, some reported complete recovery from previously entrenched illnesses. In the hands of Dr. Travumov and Dr. Kaznachive, this technology emerged as a potential catalyst for elevating human consciousness, heralding a breakthrough that, if wielded responsibly, could redefine the human experience.

However, the extraordinary capabilities unearthed by Kozyrev mirrors came with a cautious caveat. The scientists, in tandem with the apprehensive CIA, recognized the inherent dangers of activating superhuman abilities. A profound responsibility accompanied the potential to reshape human cognition. Yet, as the researchers delved deeper, they unearthed a dimension of concern that extended beyond the bounds of caution.

In the cosmic tapestry of Kozyrev space, participants discovered they were not solitary explorers. The more time spent within, the more collective experiences unfolded. Astonishingly, 75 percent reported sightings of UFOs, 70 percent beheld extraterrestrial structures, and 68 percent felt the palpable presence of entities described as The Observers. These ethereal beings, luminous and humanoid yet distinctly non-human, entered the narrative of Kozyrev space, earning the moniker "The Observers."

For many, encounters with The Observers elicited discomfort that veered into fear. Participants described chilling sensations, cold touches on their necks, and an overwhelming sense of being watched. The Observers, bathed in radiant light, manifested as enigmatic figures devoid of discernible features. Intriguingly, these entities demonstrated the ability to physically interact with those within Kozyrev space, leaving a palpable imprint on the participants' consciousness.

In certain instances, communication between the mirrors became a conduit for dialogue with The Observers. Participants recounted moments of inquiry, seeking to unravel the identity of these luminous entities. The responses, or lack thereof, added layers of mystery to the encounters. Human shapes and radiant lights flickered within the cosmic expanse, blurring the boundaries between the known and the enigmatic.

As the interplay between human consciousness and The Observers unfolded, the Kozyrev mirrors became portals not only to heightened abilities but also to encounters with entities that transcended the ordinary bounds of reality. The exploration of Kozyrev space ventured into the realm of the extraordinary, where the boundaries between observer and observed blurred in the luminous tapestry of this ethereal journey.

◆ ◆ ◆

CHAPTER 8: COMMUNING WITH THE OBSERVERS

A Glimpse Beyond the Veil

As participants continued their exploration of Kozyrev space, encounters with The Observers unfolded as intricate, unsettling dialogues. Attempting to engage with these luminous entities, participants sought answers to the fundamental question of identity. In the ethereal expanse, the response echoed enigma — an unidentified luminosity that transcended the familiar contours of human features.

Communication with The Observers proved to be an unsettling odyssey for most. A participant recounted a moment of inquiry, seeking to unravel the essence of these entities. The exchange unfolded in a realm where conventional queries met cryptic responses. An interplay of lights, shapes, and a haunting voice raised more questions than answers. The participant, expressing a desire to meet The Observers, received a cryptic response, leaving an indelible imprint of uncertainty.

For many, encounters with The Observers delved into disconcerting territories. Visions materialized, featuring devices adorned with lights and enigmatic objects. Participants, teetering on the edge of fear, grappled with entities that proclaimed their formlessness — beings that declared themselves as nothing and everything simultaneously. The unsettling gaze of eyes devoid of kindness added layers of mystique to the experience.

In an unexpected twist, some participants not only beheld UFOs in the sky but found themselves within these unidentified flying crafts. One account unfolded within a black hemisphere, where opened doors revealed beings of smaller stature. The questioning that ensued yielded responses hinting at a passive observation of humanity from a distant star.

Amid these encounters, a particularly unsettling prediction emerged. An Observer, shrouded in the enigma of a faceless form, conveyed a foreboding message. In a room unseen before, a voice spoke of danger befalling Earth, cautioning against excessive immersion in the mirrors. The prophecy, delivered with deliberate slowness, hinted at an impending disaster, leaving the participant grappling with uncertainty about the nature and timeline of the envisioned catastrophe.

The revelations within Kozyrev space transcended mere glimpses of the future; for over 40 percent of participants, they ventured into the uncharted realm of time travel. These experiences, diverse in nature, unfolded as individuals found themselves revisiting various junctures of their lives. Some observed their existence unfold like a cinematic reel, while others actively engaged in and reshaped their past.

The spectrum of temporal exploration expanded further, encompassing narratives of individuals who claimed to have witnessed or actively participated in historical events. A woman recounted her role as an advisor to Genghis Khan, while another described a consciousness transfer to someone amidst the Middle Ages. The unfolding scenes of the Roman Empire became a vivid tableau for another participant. These tales aligned with Nikolai Kosarev's vision — that time, akin to energy, could encode and transmit information, especially during transformative states like the shifting phases of water.

The choice of the Dixon site, nestled in permafrost, bore significance in this context. Researchers hypothesized that the frozen expanse of the Arctic, encapsulating information within its icy confines, might serve as a wellspring of time energy. The thawing process, they believed, unleashed this reservoir of temporal information, providing a conduit for those attuned to Kozyrev space.

While this groundbreaking research unfolded, mainstream science journals in the West remained reticent, denying it the acknowledgment it deserved. Despite the commendable strides achieved under the auspices of the Soviet and Russian governments, the scientific community's reluctance to embrace the Kozyrev mirrors persisted. Only the CIA, in recently declassified documents, revealed its vigilant observation of this unconventional exploration.

In the past couple of years, a surge of interest emanated from these clandestine records, breathing newfound life into the forgotten saga of Kozyrev mirrors. As the revelations continue to captivate minds, the enigma surrounding these mirrors, their potential, and the uncharted realms of temporal exploration linger as an invitation to unravel the mysteries hidden within the folds of time itself. For those intrigued by this narrative, the linked resources below offer a deeper dive into the uncharted territories explored by Doctors Kaznachieve and Travamov.

◆ ◆ ◆

CHAPTER 9: UNLOCKING MYSTERIES

The Enigmatic Journey of Kozyrev Mirrors

While the scientific community has largely brushed aside the tantalizing revelations stemming from the Kozyrev mirrors, recent disclosures from the CIA suggest a covert interest in this unexplored territory. Over the past couple of years, the CIA has declassified documents indicating not only their meticulous tracking of Kozyrev mirror research but also potential endeavors into their own investigations. One elusive document in the CIA database delves into the mirrors' capacity to unveil human psychic abilities and awaken consciousness, remaining classified despite numerous Freedom of Information requests.

The Siberian research conducted in the '90s by Dr. Kazanachieve and Dr. Trevumov, as detailed in their publications and interviews, is a captivating tale. The legitimacy of these accounts is a challenging puzzle to unravel. On one side, mainstream science dismisses the entire narrative, while on the other, intelligence agencies show keen interest. The researchers, funded by the Soviet state during the early stages of their work, have little incentive to fabricate their findings.

The technology associated with Kozyrev mirrors is not entirely elusive; one can acquire them or even build one using available blueprints. Despite the accessibility, the technology remains on the fringes, prompting questions about its widespread adoption. While the materials needed are not prohibitively expensive, the technology's unconventional nature might contribute to its limited acceptance.

Central to this debate is Nikolai Kozyrev's theory, which hinges on the existence of time energy and The Ether. The term "The Ether" faces skepticism within mainstream science, yet parallels can be drawn to concepts like dark matter or quantum foam. Historical instances exist where ideas initially rejected gained scientific validation. The question lingers: What if Kozyrev's theories about time energy align with these paradigms?

The boundary between science fiction and reality blurred recently when scientists at the Advanced Science Research Center at the City University of New York conducted a groundbreaking experiment. They successfully sent an electromagnetic wave through a meta-material, revealing a Time reflection—a phenomenon theorized by Nikolai Kozyrev.

This experimental validation challenges our conventional understanding of linear time, confirming that time is not as straightforward as we once believed.

Kozyrev's insights extend beyond the theoretical realm, as Dr. Travamov has applied his theories to earthquake prediction with surprising success. While earthquake prediction typically boasts an average accuracy of eight percent, Travamov achieved an impressive 61 percent accuracy in 2018 using Kozyrev mirrors. This hints at the technology's potential applications in foreseeing dangerous weather, volcanic eruptions, and even solar storms.

The versatile capabilities of Kozyrev mirrors don't stop there. According to Travamov and Kaznachieve, this technology could revolutionize our approach to various fields. From studying our solar system and deep space to aiding the search for extraterrestrial civilizations, the mirrors offer a unique perspective. Furthermore, their potential extends to slowing down the aging process and curing currently incurable diseases, opening doors to groundbreaking advancements in medical science.

Despite these remarkable possibilities, mainstream science remains hesitant to embrace Kozyrev mirrors fully. Travelmov and Kaznachieve advocate for democratizing this technology, making it accessible to everyone. They express concerns about potential misuse by governments or corporations and emphasize the importance of shared knowledge for the benefit of humanity.

Kozyrev's overarching message challenges the notion of fate and determinism, highlighting our collective potential to shape our reality through choices and actions. It underscores the interconnectedness of all living beings and the universe through subtle fields of energy and information.

In the face of these revelations, the choice becomes clear: either democratize this transformative technology, enabling widespread access and knowledge exchange, or risk its confinement to classified realms controlled by entities like the CIA. The decision is pivotal, and the potential for a collective evolutionary leap forward is too significant to ignore.

So, as plans for the weekend unfold, some might find themselves at Home Depot, eager to explore the possibilities that Kozyrev mirrors hold. After all, the pursuit of knowledge and empowerment knows no bounds.

◆ ◆ ◆

PART 3: JOURNEY TO INFINITY

Decoding the Gateway Experience

INTRODUCTION

In the quest for superior military capabilities, the United States military has delved into various realms of experimentation. From performance-enhancing drugs to mind-altering substances, and even brain implant technology, the pursuit of creating the ultimate soldier knows no bounds. However, a pivotal moment in this exploration occurred in 1983 when Lieutenant Colonel Wayne McDonald submitted an extraordinary report to US Army intelligence titled "Analysis and Assessment of Gateway Process."

This report wasn't just another military experiment; it was a detailed guide on achieving an out-of-body experience specifically for intelligence gathering purposes. But McDonald's revelations went far beyond the realms of traditional military experimentation. According to the report, advanced participants in the Gateway process could transcend the limitations of our reality. They could not only project their consciousness to different locations but completely exit the construct of our universe. Through this process, individuals could traverse the universe, visiting any point in time.

In a shocking twist, the Gateway report proposed that our universe might not be as concrete as it seems. Instead, it suggested that our reality is a construct created by the mind. The Gateway process offered a means to escape this construct, allowing individuals to perceive the true nature of reality. Despite its groundbreaking potential, the 30-page Gateway report was promptly classified, primarily due to its democratizing nature – anyone, including you, could learn to embark on this extraordinary journey.

Embark on a riveting exploration as we delve into the secrets concealed within the Gateway process, uncovering the mysteries of consciousness, reality, and the boundless potential that lies beyond the veil.

❖ ❖ ❖

CHAPTER 1: DECODING THE CLASSIFIED GATEWAY REPORT

Colonel McDonald's "Analysis and Assessment of Gateway Process" gets straight to the point: there are alternate states of reality and other dimensions that exist beyond our physical world and outside of time itself. If this sounds paranormal or like new age mysticism, you're not alone. Even Colonel McDonnell acknowledged that this might be the impression his report would give. Surprisingly, this remains one of the strangest military reports, and it's remarkable that it's not still classified.

According to the report, we can use the Gateway process to access other dimensions. To ground his research in science, McDonald consulted Itzak Bentov, a respected biomedical engineer, to understand the physical aspects of the process. Quantum mechanics is employed to describe the nature of human consciousness, and both classical and theoretical physics are used to explain the out-of-body phenomenon.

Most crucially, the report provides step-by-step instructions on how to have a Gateway experience. By following these instructions, one can learn to project their consciousness, visit other dimensions, and even navigate through the fabric of time itself.

Navigating Other Realms with the Gateway Process

The instructions provided in the report enable individuals to learn how to project their consciousness, visit other dimensions, and even maneuver through the fabric of time. This unique ability drew the attention of the military, leading to years of extensive study. Imagine a unit of psychic spies trained to project their consciousness anywhere unnoticed—an incredibly effective method for intelligence gathering.

While McDonald was aware that his report would be met with skepticism, he firmly believed in the feasibility of the Gateway process. He asserted that there was a rational basis in terms of physical science parameters for considering Gateway plausible in achieving its essential objectives. He saw the potential for intuitive insights of personal and practical nature, making it a reasonable expectation.

The Gateway process, developed in the 1970s by the Monroe Institute in Virginia, offers a week-long training that anyone, even today, can undergo. However, the report concluded with an unexpected warning. As this method is accessible to anyone, Colonel McDonnell cautioned that the military should be prepared for encounters with intelligent beings.

Despite the accessibility of the Gateway method to anyone, Colonel McDonnell issued a warning to the military about potential encounters with intelligent and non-friendly entities beyond the boundaries of time and space. This implied the possibility of a psychic war. Learning the Gateway method is not a quick fix; it requires foundational work. Relaxation techniques, meditation, and extreme focus are prerequisites. Moreover, one must set aside doubt and embrace a new way of thinking.

As the saying goes, "ain't no such thing as a free lunch." Mastering the Gateway method involves learning these techniques before delving into the true nature of reality. The foundational idea is that everything, including life, Earth, and the universe, is an illusion created by the mind. Solid matter, in the strict sense, does not exist; instead, atomic structures are composed of oscillating energy grids. These grids, vibrating at extremely fast frequencies, make up everything from the largest objects in the universe to atoms and subatomic particles —everything is energy.

◆ ◆ ◆

CHAPTER 2: THE ILLUSION OF REALITY

Everything around us, including the entire human being—brain, consciousness, and all—is essentially an extraordinarily complex system of energy fields. In essence, what we perceive as states of matter are merely variances in energy. Human consciousness, too, is a product of the interaction of energy.

Our consciousness is finely tuned into specific frequencies of energy that make up the world we perceive. However, it's essential to recognize that we only grasp a small percentage of the energy that surrounds us. Analogous to tuning a radio, where you hear only the music broadcast on the specific channel you've selected, our brains filter out everything except the energy that constructs our reality. Like a radio converting energy into sound, our brains transform this universal energy into the sensory experiences of sight, sound, taste, and touch. The solid matter we perceive is not actually present; our senses generate the illusion of matter to make our reality comprehensible.

The Gateway report contends that our existence is within a shared universal hologram, a vast and intricate construct composed of interacting energy fields. According to the theories proposed by Carl Prebroom, a neuroscientist at Stanford University, and David Boom, a physicist at the University of London, the human mind itself functions as a hologram. This mental hologram attunes itself to the universal hologram, resulting in the state we recognize as consciousness.

Intriguingly, the Gateway process proposes a method to bypass the usual filters in the brain. By doing so, individuals can gain access to alternate states of reality and transcend the constraints of space and time. Remarkably, this process is accessible to anyone; no esoteric practices, mind-altering substances, or lengthy spiritual journeys are required. All you need are headphones.

The Gateway process relies on the use of sound. In the 1950s, Robert Monroe, a New York broadcasting executive, discovered that different sound patterns could have distinct effects on the human mind. Some sounds induce sleepiness, while others promote alertness. Certain sounds can evoke anxiety, while others induce relaxation. In this process, the key tool is sound—specifically designed audio sequences that guide individuals into altered states of consciousness. So, forget about decalcifying your pineal gland or embarking on prolonged spiritual pursuits; with the Gateway process, all you need is the power of sound through your headphones.

As Monroe listened to the sound frequency, an unusual progression unfolded. His body gradually succumbed to paralysis, accompanied by a building vibration that intensified. Suddenly, he found himself engulfed in a brilliant white light. A subsequent rush of air, almost like a deafening roar, overwhelmed him. Then, in an instant, silence descended. The vibration ceased, the light dissipated, and Monroe discovered himself floating above his own sleeping body—an experience later coined as an out-of-body experience (OBE), a term popularized by Monroe himself.

◆ ◆ ◆

CHAPTER 3: HARMONY OF HEMISPHERES

Synchronizing Brain States at the Monroe Institute

In the wake of his extraordinary out-of-body experiences, Robert Monroe chronicled his journey in the 1971 book "Journeys Out of the Body." Motivated by these encounters, Monroe established the Monroe Institute, emerging as a notable figure in the exploration of human consciousness.

Through his continued exploration, Monroe made a groundbreaking discovery: while in an out-of-body state, he could identify, access, and sustain different states of consciousness. This feat relied on the synchronization of the left and right hemispheres of the brain, a process integral to the methodology developed at the Monroe Institute.

In the pursuit of unlocking the mind's potential, the Gateway process employs a technique called Hemi Sync, likened to harmonizing the brain's two hemispheres—a dance between the logical left and the creative right. This synchronization occurs through a fundamental practice known as Hemi-Sync, a cornerstone of the Gateway Experience.

The human brain, with its diverse functions split between the left and right hemispheres, operates at different frequencies. The left hemisphere, associated with logic and cognitive control, hums along in the beta frequency range (13 to 30 Hertz). Meanwhile, the right hemisphere, fostering relaxation, creativity, and spatial processing, resonates in the alpha frequency range (8 to 13 Hertz), a slower tempo compared to its counterpart.

In the Gateway process, participants engage in Hemisync to bring enhanced strength, focus, and coherence to the brain's wave output, creating a synchronized dance between the two hemispheres. This synchronization is not just a balancing act; it's a transformative experience designed to alter consciousness, ultimately transcending the confines of the physical realm and liberating the mind from the constraints of time and space.

The Gateway report aptly describes Hemi Sync as the shift from a chaotic, uneven lamp-like emission of light to a laser-like precision. Through this process, the mind, operating with focused energy, gains access to various levels of intuitive knowledge embedded in the vast expanse of the universe.

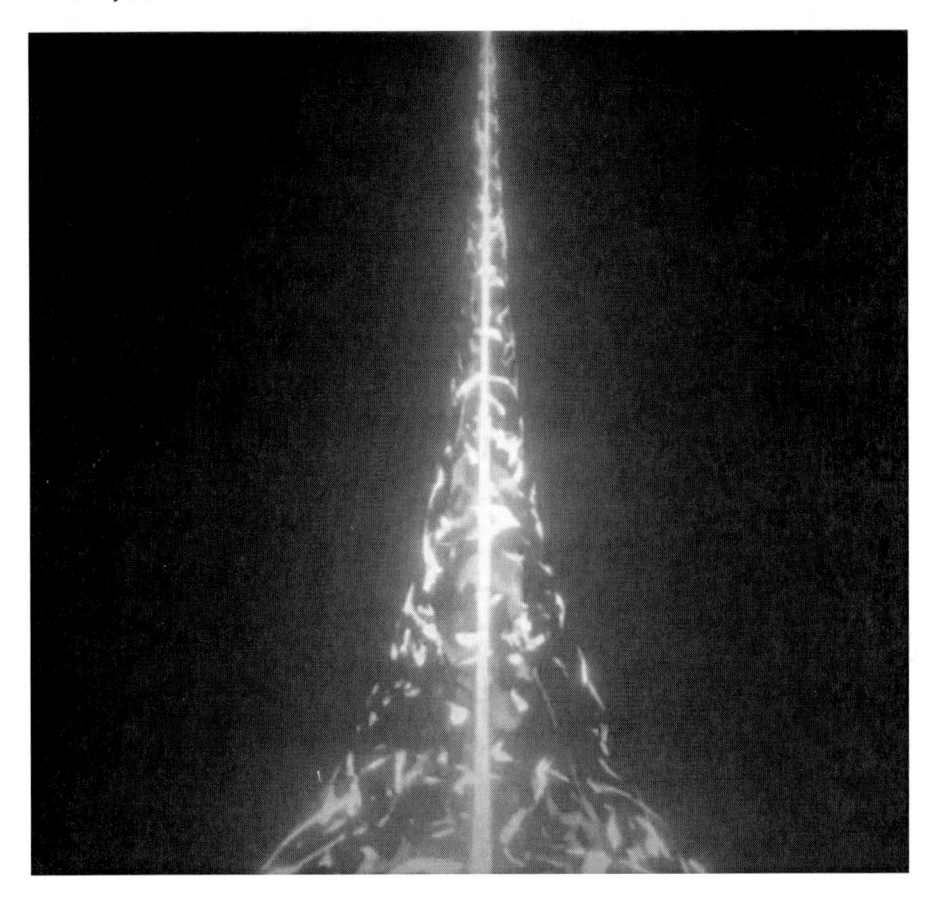

As the frequencies and amplitudes of the human brain align, the vibrational levels of the mind ascend. In this heightened state, the mind synchronizes with the intricate energy levels of the universe. At these elevated levels, the mind becomes a sophisticated processor capable of navigating and interpreting the complex tapestry of cosmic energy.

Figure B Diagram of the Cosmic Egg

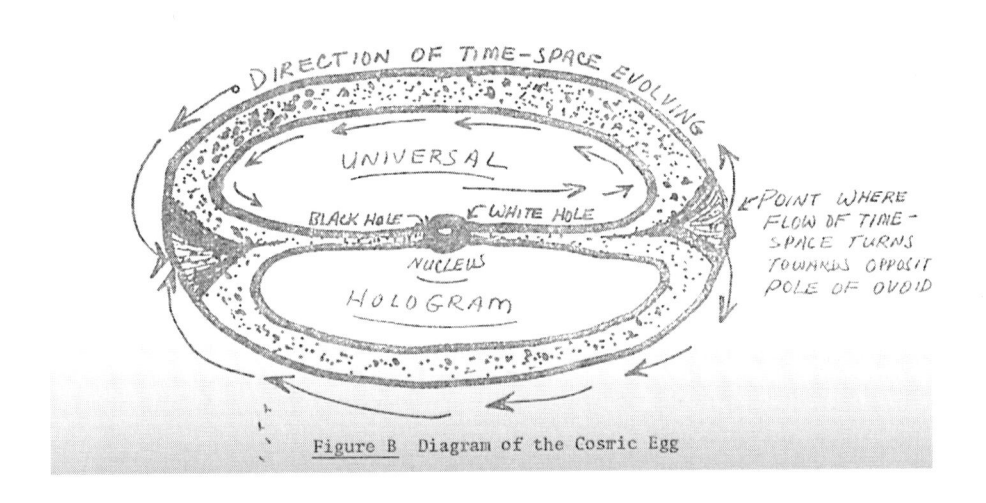

Mastering the Matrix: The Holographic Realm

In the quest to unravel the mysteries of the mind, the Gateway process ventures into the realm of holographic theory —a journey that promises not just understanding but the ability to wield reality itself. Colonel McDonald's Gateway report introduces us to the holographic principle, a key to comprehending how human consciousness can transcend the confines of the physical body.

Holographic theory, as outlined in the report, revolves around the idea that energy projects or expands at specific frequencies, creating a three-dimensional living pattern known as a hologram. This holographic projection is not a mere illusion but a dynamic encoding of immense detail. To illustrate this concept, the report delves into a mind-bending example: creating a holographic projection of a glass of swamp water. Astonishingly, if one were to examine the holographic projection (not the water itself) under a microscope, microscopic organisms would come to life as intricate holographic representations. As the report unfolds, it contends that holograms have the capacity to encode an extraordinary amount of detail, down to the microscopic level. This revelation taps into the core principle that the universe's meaning is intricately woven through holographic projections.

The CIA, recognizing the significance of these revelations, embraced the exploration of holographic principles. The Gateway report draws a parallel to the concept of simulation theory, where the late John Wheeler's delayed-choice experiment becomes a crucial reference. This experiment, explored in a previous episode on simulation theory, hinted at the malleable nature of reality—a notion that finds resonance in the Gateway process.

Riding the Waves of Information

As we plunge deeper into the Gateway process, Colonel McDonald's report beckons us to contemplate the very fabric of our universe. Building upon the groundwork laid by John Wheeler's delayed-choice double-slit experiment and the profound insights of simulation theory, the Gateway report introduces us to the captivating realm of holographic theory.

Wheeler's experiment hinted at particles exhibiting the ability to alter their state by seemingly traversing time—a revelation that fueled Wheeler's belief that the universe is fundamentally composed of information, not merely matter and energy. In essence, the holographic theory posits that our three-dimensional universe is a product of information, a concept widely embraced by theoretical physicists.

The Gateway report underscores the established status of holographic theory in physics, emphasizing its acceptance within the scientific community. To comprehend the intricacies of this theory, one must grapple with the idea that the universe's composition is not confined to matter and energy but extends into the realm of information.

However, the Gateway report extends this concept beyond the boundaries of our known universe, daring to suggest that information exchange can transcend dimensions. This proposition opens a portal to uncharted territories, hinting at the existence of dimensions yet to be unveiled.

❖ ❖ ❖

CHAPTER 4: CLICKING OUT OF REALITY

Unleashing the Power of Consciousness

In the ever-expanding tapestry of the Gateway process, Colonel McDonald's insights propel us into the profound realm of consciousness and its dynamic interaction with the holographic universe. The question at the forefront: Can our consciousness, a potent form of energy, engage in a cosmic exchange of information with dimensions beyond our comprehension?

The Gateway process responds with an affirmative nod, asserting that human beings are not mere passive recipients of universal information. Rather, we are active participants, intricately woven into the fabric of the information that shapes our reality. McDonald introduces us to the transformative concept of "patterning," a technique that empowers us to not only perceive but also influence and mold the very reality we inhabit.

Patterning acknowledges the pivotal role of consciousness as the wellspring of all reality. It contends that our thoughts possess a unique potency, capable of exerting influence on the reality that unfolds around us. Imagine the resonance with the popular notions of the Law of Attraction and the concept of the Secret, where the focus of our thoughts manifests tangible outcomes in our lives.

Yet, the Gateway process doesn't stop at envisioning the power of consciousness; it guides us on a journey to understand how to unlock this potential. The Planck distance, a minute unit of length at 1.6 times 10 to the negative 35 meters, serves as the focal point of speculation. This infinitesimal scale challenges the conventional laws of physics, suggesting a boundary where our understanding falters.

In the mesmerizing realm of the Gateway process, Colonel McDonald beckons us to explore the frontiers of consciousness, proposing a tantalizing possibility—accelerating brainwave frequencies to transcend the very limitations set by the Planck distance. The outcome, he suggests, is an ephemeral departure from human perception, a fleeting moment known as "clicking out of reality." Within this infinitesimal window, consciousness aligns with the boundless expanse of Infinity.

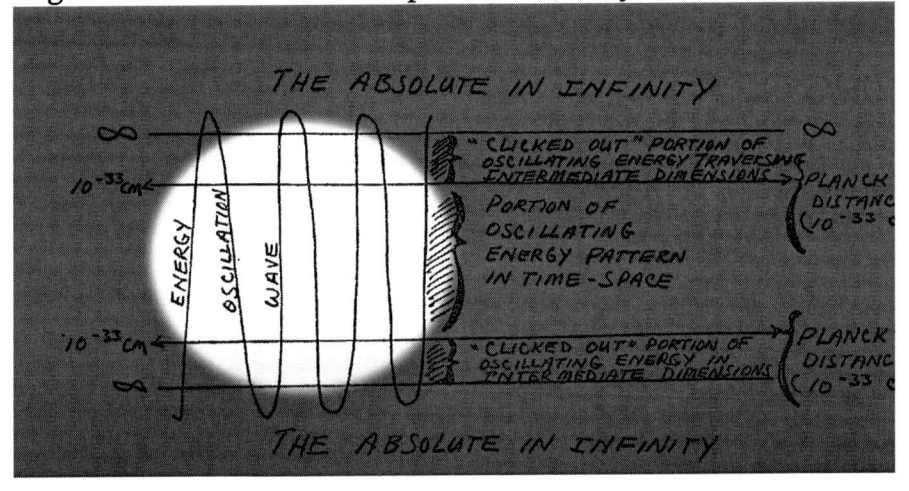

The crux of this transcendental journey lies in understanding the Planck distance, a minuscule measure where conventional laws of physics falter. McDonald speculates that when the oscillation speed drops below this critical threshold, consciousness momentarily escapes the confines of time and space, merging with the infinite.

Bent off, a luminary in quantum mechanics, adds weight to this proposition, stating that as distances approach or go below Planck's distance, a new world emerges, challenging our conventional understanding of reality. It is within this uncharted territory that the Gateway process beckons, inviting us to traverse the boundary between the known and the unknown.

Yet, fear not, for our journey remains firmly rooted in the exploration of ideas rather than a literal escape from reality. Let's delve into the mechanics of the Gateway process, demystifying its techniques. The program seamlessly weaves two methodologies to orchestrate its transformative symphony.

The first, Frequency Following Response (FFR), introduces a frequency through headphones, coaxing the brain to mirror this input by adjusting its own brainwaves. The second technique, Beat Frequency or binaural beats, presents different frequencies in each ear. In response, the brain chooses to perceive the disparity between these frequencies. Picture this as an auditory dance, where the brain orchestrates its rhythm in harmony with the frequencies it encounters.

As we embark on this auditory adventure, remember, our goal is not to escape reality today, but to fathom the mechanics of the Gateway process. So, grab your headphones, and let's unravel the secrets that lie within the oscillations of our consciousness.

◆ ◆ ◆

CHAPTER 5: HARMONIZING FREQUENCIES

A Prelude to Perception

In our exploration of the Gateway process, we now turn our attention to the symphony of frequencies that compose this transformative experience. Picture your brain as an orchestra, with each hemisphere playing a distinct role in this auditory masterpiece.

The Gateway process employs a technique known as Beat Frequency or binaural beats, where different frequencies are presented to each ear. This prompts the brain to discern the difference between these frequencies, creating a harmonious interplay that transcends the audible spectrum. Allow me to illustrate this with an example.

As we revel in the vibrato of frequencies, remember that this dance mirrors the intricate relationship between the left and right hemispheres of the brain. The left brain, our bastion of logic and analysis, processes information, filtering and deciphering it before acceptance. On the other hand, the right brain, the domain of emotion and creativity, embraces information with open arms.

Delving into the realms of psychology, scholars like Ronald Stone shed light on the nature of hypnosis. This technique, akin to the Gateway process, relaxes or distracts the left brain, offering unimpeded access to the intuitive and creative right brain. It's in this state that individuals become highly receptive, their logical faculties temporarily disengaged.

Beyond the Looking Glass

As we embark on the Gateway process, envision your consciousness as a ship navigating the vast sea of energy waves. Our journey takes a fascinating turn as we delve into the intricacies of the almost continuous click-out pattern and the enigmatic realm beyond Planck's distance.

Picture your brain waves as the undulating waves in McDonald's drawing—a representation of our consciousness, an energy dance that propels us into uncharted territories. The Gateway process orchestrates this dance by relaxing the left brain through the mesmerizing cadence of sound waves. As the brain succumbs to this rhythmic lullaby, the amplitude and frequency of brain waves ascend, and the interwave spaces contract.

The captivating phenomenon that occurs when the distance between brain waves drops below Planck's distance. It's like Alice beginning her journey into Wonderland—a Wonderland where everything is energy, where the boundaries of time and space blur into a cosmic dance.

The Gateway process propels us through the looking glass of time-space, where our consciousness takes on a surreal quality. In this state of continuous phase, we transcend the limitations of conventional reality. Imagine it as a brief sojourn into the timeless expanse, a momentary escape from the constraints of our familiar universe.

As we navigate this ethereal landscape, keep in mind that, at its core, everything is energy. Whether you label it brain waves, energy waves, or consciousness, the essence remains the same. Our journey through the Gateway is a testament to the malleability of reality—a journey into the profound mysteries that lie beyond the looking glass.

◆ ◆ ◆

CHAPTER 6: THE CLICK-OUT POINT

Where Waves Meet Infinity

The mesmerizing concept of the click-out point—the juncture where our consciousness, energy waves, or brain waves transition from the material reality we perceive to the infinite expanse of the absolute.

Imagine the wave as a cosmic dance, a perpetual ebb, and flow of energy. The middle of the wave, where it spends the majority of its time, encapsulates our familiar reality—the world we see, touch, and navigate daily. However, the magic unfolds at the extremities—the peaks and troughs, where the wave momentarily comes to a standstill.

In those fleeting instances just before the wave changes direction—before it ascends or descends—something extraordinary happens. It clicks out of our conventional reality and, as per the Gateway report, merges with infinity and the absolute energy. Physicists term this state as energy in its absolute form, a realm beyond the boundaries of our perceived universe.

Picture it as a brief pause in the cosmic dance, a moment frozen in the dance of the universe. This inactive infinity, this absolute state of energy, permeates every dimension, including the time-space dimension that constitutes our physical existence. Yet, it remains elusive to our perception.

To simplify, envision our reality as the top layer, the tangible world we inhabit. Beneath it lie mysterious dimensions, and underneath them all is the absolute, as described by McDonald. It's a layered existence, with our reality resting atop these unseen dimensions, all supported by the foundational absolute.

McDonald's intricate depiction might seem complex, but at its essence, it's an exploration of the interplay between our reality and the boundless infinity that underlies it.

The Absolute: You, Me, and the Conscious Energy Field

Now, let's unravel the enigma of the absolute—a conscious energy field at rest, omnipresent but unseen, shaping our reality and the dimensions beyond. In simpler terms, imagine the absolute as the canvas on which the masterpiece of our existence unfolds.

The absolute, as McDonald describes it, is like the backdrop to a play, omnipresent but often overlooked. It's an energy field at rest, doing nothing but providing the stage for the dance of dimensions, including our own. Think of it as the ultimate source, the energy field that birthed everything, yet remains serene and unaffected.

So, who created the absolute? In a surprising twist, it's not an external force but us—every individual, collectively contributing to the grand tapestry of existence. The absolute is the canvas, and we are the brushstrokes, creating our reality and the diverse dimensions that coexist within it.

In the journey of life, we're born into this tangible reality, each with our unique consciousness. As we traverse our time on Earth, experiencing the richness of existence, there comes a moment when our individual consciousness returns to the absolute. According to the Gateway report, this return is not a dissolution but a reunion with a collective consciousness. Here's where it gets intriguing—we retain our individual identities even in this collective embrace, suggesting a form of immortality.

Colonel McDonald posits that the absolute could be perceived as what many might call God—an all-encompassing consciousness that intertwines with our individual selves, a concept of divinity rooted in the fabric of our own creation.

Colonel McDonald's profound interpretation of the absolute—a concept that echoes across various religious philosophies, from Hebrew mysticism to the Christian Trinity and even Eastern teachings. In McDonald's perspective, the absolute is akin to what many conceive as God—an omnipotent, omniscient divinity, shrouded in unknowable mystery in its primary state of being.

The idea of the absolute at rest in Infinity finds resonance in Hebrew mystical philosophy, where the visible reality is seen as an emanation of a divine force beyond human comprehension. The Christian concept of the Trinity, with its threefold nature, also finds echoes in McDonald's description of the absolute.

To substantiate his theories, McDonald draws from diverse sources, including Tibetan teachings and ancient Hindu texts, underlining the universality of the absolute across different belief systems.

Moving beyond religious boundaries, McDonald then explores the nature of the absolute itself and how it achieves self-awareness. According to his insights, the absolute, in order to attain self-consciousness, projects a hologram of itself and perceives it. In this framework, the absolute becomes the ultimate force behind all creation, shaping reality and giving rise to the eternal thought or concept of self.

This profound understanding, as Colonel McDonald asserts, unifies diverse belief systems. Regardless of individual beliefs, the core concept remains the same—we are all part of a shared reality created by the absolute.

◆ ◆ ◆

CHAPTER 7: REVEALING THE MISSING PAGE AND GATEWAY'S UNIVERSAL PURPOSE

As we conclude our journey through the Gateway process, we encounter a mysterious missing page, page 25, which the CIA claimed not to possess. However, recent revelations in 2021, spurred by public pressure and inquiries, led to the release of the complete Gateway report, including the enigmatic page.

On this final page, Colonel McDonald encapsulates the essence of the Gateway process. Contrary to religious and cultural boundaries, McDonald asserts that the Gateway process serves as a universal tool, transcending divisions and offering a profound understanding of oneself and the nature of the universe.

Drawing parallels with ancient mystics who intuited fundamental truths about the cosmos, McDonald suggests that the Gateway process aligns with these timeless insights. According to his perspective, every individual on Earth is interconnected, contributing to a collective consciousness. This interconnectedness is purposeful—an amalgamation of diverse experiences and shared learning, all aimed at accumulating knowledge.

McDonald invites us to recognize a shared purpose—to learn

from one another, accumulate wisdom, and, ultimately, carry that knowledge back to the universal energy from whence we came. In essence, the Gateway process becomes a guide for understanding the interconnected tapestry of human existence, transcending the boundaries of time, culture, and individual beliefs.

As we reflect on McDonald's profound insights, the Gateway process emerges not just as a military experiment but as a potential catalyst for personal and universal enlightenment, inviting us to delve into the depths of our collective consciousness and the boundless mysteries of the cosmos.

Practical Applications of the Gateway Process

The final segment of Colonel McDonald's report, the focus returns to the practical applications of the Gateway process within the realm of military strategy and intelligence gathering. Despite the overarching theme of unity and interconnectedness, McDonald shifts gears to address the specific steps the military could take to harness the potential of out-of-body experiences.

McDonald recommends a phased approach for military personnel interested in implementing the Gateway process. The first phase involves utilizing Gateway tapes to learn the technique of hemi sync, a process aimed at synchronizing brainwaves. This foundational step sets the stage for trainees to understand how to induce altered states of consciousness effectively.

Moving into the second phase, trainees are encouraged to master the art of inducing these altered states at will. This level of proficiency becomes crucial as it lays the groundwork for the ultimate objective: achieving an out-of-body experience.

The out-of-body experience is positioned as a valuable tool, particularly for remote viewing—a method employed for gathering intelligence. McDonald envisions military personnel learning to project their consciousness to remote locations, enabling them to access information that would otherwise be difficult to obtain through conventional means.

This practical aspect of the Gateway process, it becomes evident that McDonald, despite his military background, sees the potential benefits beyond strategic advantages. There's a subtle acknowledgment that the Gateway process could genuinely help individuals, transcending its initial military intent.

Reflections on the Gateway Process

It's time to reflect on the practical applications proposed by Colonel McDonald. While his personal trustworthiness is implied, skepticism arises when considering the broader context of the United States military wielding such knowledge. The idea of adjusting reality for what McDonald terms "practical applications" raises eyebrows and prompts contemplation about the ethical implications of introducing such techniques into military strategy.

McDonald's genuine belief in the transformative power of the Gateway process is evident as he extends practical advice to those embarking on this journey. The emphasis on self-knowledge and the removal of personal biases suggests a holistic approach, encouraging individuals to grow beyond their limitations.

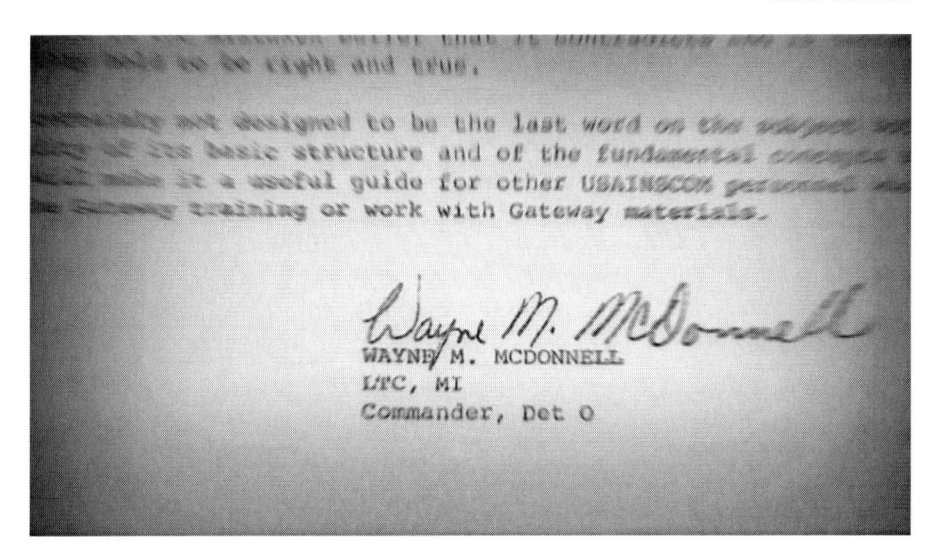

> ...known...for that it currently exists and
> ...holds to be right and true.
>
> ...not designed to be the last word on the subject...
> ...its basic structure and of the fundamental concepts...
> ...a useful guide for other USAINSCOM personnel...
> ...Gateway training or work with Gateway materials.
>
> *Wayne M. McDonnell*
> WAYNE M. MCDONNELL
> LTC, MI
> Commander, Det O

However, the inherent tension surfaces when contemplating whether the military, an entity historically associated with conflict and defense, should possess tools that could potentially manipulate reality. The optimism expressed in hoping that soldiers, as they delve into altered states of consciousness, discover the unity of the universe rather than perpetuating conflict, remains an idealistic perspective.

In the real world, optimism often contends with disappointment, and the question lingers: Can organizations driven by national defense truly embrace the underlying message of unity embedded in the Gateway process. One cannot ignore the overarching question posed by the Gateway process itself—whether it is groundbreaking insight or mere new age speculation. The dichotomy between these perspectives prompts us to consider the possibility that our current reality is just one facet of a more intricate and interconnected existence.

In the end, as we step out of the realm of military strategy and into the broader realm of human understanding, the Gateway process beckons us to ponder the nature of our existence, inviting us to explore realms beyond the tangible and challenge our perceptions of reality.

❖ ❖ ❖

CHAPTER 8: NAVIGATING THE UNKNOWN

Bridging Science and Spirituality

As we contemplate the Gateway process, the question of its validity persists—is it a transformative exploration of reality or mere new age speculation? Can we, with training and patience, unlock dimensions beyond our current understanding? Before considering these questions, it's crucial to acknowledge the risks associated with altering one's state of consciousness.

Many who have delved into the Gateway process report positive outcomes, citing increased self-awareness, creativity, and clarity in their daily lives. However, it is equally essential to recognize the potential pitfalls. Some individuals have experienced intense anxiety, depression, and, in rare cases, psychosis. The delicate balance between expanded consciousness and detachment from reality underscores the inherent risks.

Colonel McDonald's recommendation for the military to pursue the Gateway process adds a layer of complexity. While the potential benefits could enhance cognitive abilities and offer a unique perspective for strategic purposes, the ethical considerations and the possibility of unintended consequences cannot be ignored.

As we ponder these aspects, it becomes evident that McDonald, now in his 80s and long retired, has not revisited the Gateway process in his writings. One wonders if he still believes in its potential or if he ever personally experienced the realms it promises to unlock.

A desire to engage in dialogue with Colonel McDonald, to glean insights from his perspective today, lingers. Understanding whether he views the Gateway process as a groundbreaking exploration or an experiment with unknown consequences could shed light on its enduring mystery.

We confront a paradox—on one hand, the allure of unlocking hidden dimensions beckons, and on the other, the cautionary tales of those who have become untethered from reality echo. The Gateway process remains an enigma, inviting contemplation on the boundaries of our understanding and the uncharted territories that may lie beyond.

The desire to delve into the mind of Colonel McDonald intensifies as we contemplate the profound questions surrounding the Gateway process. The curiosity about whether he believes in its transformative potential or has personally traversed its uncharted territories persists.

Does he harbor a fear of death, a fear shared by many, or does the knowledge of the next realm provide him with a sense of peace? One might wonder if he envisions the absolute as a destination for the Collective Consciousness, contributing individual experiences to a universal tapestry.

In contemplating the Gateway process, a parallel emerges between its concepts and traditional notions of heaven and God. While the traditional religious perspective may differ, the idea of a collective source, an infinite Consciousness, and the return of energy to the absolute bears a resemblance to the concept of an afterlife. It raises the question: Could the Gateway process, rooted in scientific exploration, inadvertently offer evidence for the existence of a higher power or an afterlife?

The divergence between science and faith is well-established, with scientists seeking empirical evidence while the faithful rely on belief. However, what if, in the exploration of altered states of consciousness, science and spirituality converge? Could the Gateway process, with its potential to unlock hidden dimensions, serve as a bridge between these seemingly disparate realms?

As we navigate the intersection of science and spirituality, we are faced with the tantalizing prospect that they might be two facets of the same truth. Imagine a world where scientific inquiry and spiritual understanding align, where the pursuit of knowledge leads not to conflict but to a harmonious coexistence of empirical evidence and faith.

The aspiration is to discover whether the Gateway process, in its exploration of the unknown, offers insights that resonate with both scientific minds and those seeking spiritual meaning. The journey toward understanding the uncharted territories of consciousness continues, with the hope that it may reveal a shared truth, embracing the infinite potential that lies at the intersection of science and spirituality.

❖ ❖ ❖

PART 4: CHRONICLES OF TIME

The Curious Case of Sergey Panamerenko

INTRODUCTION

In the spring of 2006, in the bustling city of Kiev, Ukraine, an unusual event unfolded. Picture this: a young man, barely in his early twenties, stood near a towering apartment building. Onlookers noticed a perplexed and anxious expression on his face, mistaking him for a lost tourist. Approaching two police officers, the young man sought directions to a place that seemed to exist only in his mind. However, his identification raised eyebrows—issued by the long-gone Soviet Union, and indicating a birth date from the distant 1932.

This enigmatic figure was Sergey Panamerenko, the focal point of a Russian documentary aptly named "The Time Traveler." Witnesses were left in awe as Panamerenko appeared to slip in and out of time, clad in clothes half a century out of sync with the present.

The story begins at a Kiev intersection, where Sergey Panamerenko, in his early twenties but wearing clothing from another era, puzzled onlookers with his frantic search for "Peshnaya Street," a place unknown to anyone he encountered. As the perplexity deepened, the city's police officers, led by Sergey Annapenko, took notice, sparking an investigation into a tale that transcended the boundaries of time.

Join us on a journey through the mysterious intersections of time and space as we unravel the captivating saga of Sergey Panamerenko—a tale that challenges our understanding of reality and propels us into the realms of the unknown.

◆ ◆ ◆

CHAPTER 1: A PUZZLING ADMISSION

As Sergey Panamerenko found himself standing at the intersection, his quest for Peshnaya Street led him to a rather unexpected encounter with the keen-eyed Officer Annapenko and his partner. The confusion deepened when Sergey attempted to locate the elusive street on a map, only to discover that it seemingly existed only as a landfill.

Officer Annapenko's attention shifted to the curious details surrounding Sergey. Clad in brand-new vintage clothing, he sported an antique camera around his neck—a stark contrast to the modern surroundings. However, it was Sergey's identification that truly baffled the officer. According to the documents, Sergey was born in Kiev in 1932, making him 74 years old. Yet, the man before them appeared older than 25.

The identification papers, dated 1958, posed an even greater mystery. They were in pristine condition, raising doubts about their authenticity. Officer Annapenko, perplexed by the incongruities, couldn't reconcile the photograph on the document with the man standing before him.

Assuming that Sergey might be suffering from a mental lapse, Officer Annapenko contemplated seeking psychiatric help. Sergey, however, resisted the suggestion vehemently. Faced with the choice of psychiatric evaluation or potential arrest for vagrancy, Sergey reluctantly agreed to be taken to a private psychiatric clinic.

The subsequent events at the clinic, captured on video surveillance, added another layer of strangeness to the unfolding saga. Sergey's reluctance to seek psychiatric help hinted at a deeper mystery, leaving both officers and clinic staff puzzled by the enigma that was Sergey Panamerenko.

Whispers of the Future

As Sergey Panamerenko found himself within the confines of the psychiatric clinic, his behavior became increasingly puzzling. The clinic's receptionist recalled his arrival, noting that instead of finding clarity, Sergey seemed to descend further into confusion.

In a peculiar twist, Sergey fixated on the receptionist's mobile phone, staring at it intently. Refusing to divulge his code or surrender any of his belongings, it became evident that Sergey was going to be a challenging patient. The contrast between the man in front of them and the photograph taken at the time of his disappearance was striking—Sergey exhibited no signs of aging. Adding another layer of mystery, the background of the photograph raised eyebrows. Positioned over Sergey's right shoulder was the iconic Mother Motherland statue, unmistakably a symbol of Kiev. Investigators diligently retraced the steps to the spot where the photo was taken, confirming the location but noting discrepancies in the skyline. Kiev, it seemed, had not yet evolved to boast the skyline depicted in the photograph.

Turning to the back of the photograph, a message addressed to Valentina unfolded: "Dearest Valentina, everything is fine with me. I'll try to return when I can. Yours, Sergey." The message hinted at a journey through time, with Sergey leaping into the future once again. The enormity of Kiev in the photo, coupled with the absence of Sergey in the city up to 2011, left investigators grappling with the question of just how far into the future Sergey had ventured.

◆ ◆ ◆

CHAPTER 2: FROM FICTION TO REALITY

As Sergey Panamerenko remained elusive in the city, the resolution of this mystery seemed destined to linger in the future. Patience, it appeared, would be our greatest ally in unraveling the enigma surrounding his peculiar journey through time.

The notion of time travel has long captivated the human imagination, finding its roots in works of fiction. Louis Sebastian Mercier, in 1770, envisioned a future in "The Year 2440," where the hero traversed centuries. Charles Dickens explored time travel in "A Christmas Carol" in 1843, but it was H.G. Wells' "The Time Machine" in 1895 that truly ignited the genre.

Yet, beyond the realms of fiction, is time travel a conceivable reality? Surprisingly, the answer lies in the realm of science, particularly in the groundbreaking work of Albert Einstein. In 1905, Einstein introduced his special theory of relativity, revealing a fascinating connection between time and motion.

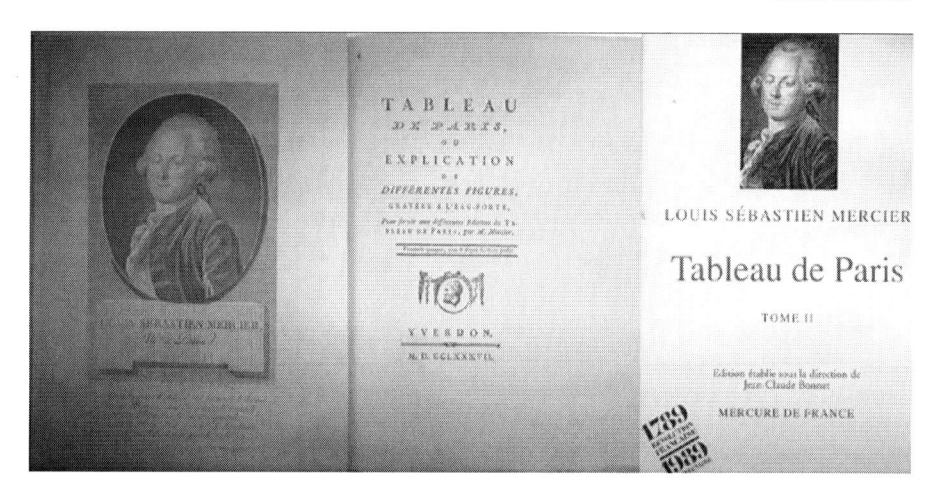

Einstein's theory proposes that moving clocks tick more slowly than stationary ones. The faster an object moves, the slower time progresses for it. This intriguing concept forms the foundation for the possibility of traveling into the future. Imagine this: board a spaceship capable of reaching 99.995% of the speed of light, embark on a journey 50 light years away, turn around, and return. Astonishingly, while a century would have passed on Earth, the fast-paced voyage would only take a year for the space traveler.

This theory, seemingly plucked from the pages of science fiction, has manifested in the real world. Conducting experiments with highly accurate clocks on planes flying in the same direction as the Earth's rotation, scientists observed a minute time discrepancy upon landing. It's a tangible glimpse into the fascinating interplay between motion and the passage of time.

Time's Bend: Einstein's Gravity Dance

So, we've ventured into Einstein's world of relativity, but let's break it down a bit. Einstein had two big theories: special relativity and general relativity.

Special Relativity: In 1905, Einstein dropped a bomb of brilliance called special relativity. Picture this: the faster you move, the slower time moves for you. It's like a cosmic speed limit. If you hopped on a super-fast spaceship and zipped around the universe, when you returned, less time would have passed for you compared to everyone back on Earth. It's like time playing catch-up.

General Relativity: In 1915, Einstein cranked it up a notch with general relativity. This theory is all about gravity bending the fabric of space-time. Think of space-time as a cosmic blanket, and gravity is like a bowling ball placed on it, causing a dip. The heavier the bowling ball (or object with gravity), the bigger the dip, and the slower time moves. This phenomenon is called gravitational time dilation.

Let's ditch the technical talk for a moment. Remember in that movie "Interstellar" with Matthew McConaughey? When they land on a planet near a black hole, time goes haywire because of crazy gravity. Every hour on the planet means seven years pass back on Earth. It's a dramatic example of gravitational time dilation.

Now, think about GPS satellites. They're way up there, about 12,000 miles above Earth. Up there, gravity is weaker, and time ticks a bit faster. But here's the catch: the clocks on those satellites need tweaking to sync up with the slower-moving time down here on Earth. It's like keeping our cosmic watches in harmony.

Chapter 6: "Unlocking the Past: Theoretical Time Travel"

Now that we've taken a spin through how time behaves in the

gravitational dance, let's shift our gaze to an even more mind-bending idea: time travel to the past. Buckle up because this gets a bit more theoretical and, dare I say, controversial.

Einstein's theories, the rockstars of physics, suggest that in theory, traveling back in time is possible. How? Picture this: imagine bending or warping space-time so much that you create a shortcut from Point A to Point B. This shortcut would let you zip through space-time faster than the speed of light, and if you can make space-time loop around itself like a cosmic cylinder, voilà, you're on a time-traveling adventure.

In this theoretical scenario, your path through time becomes a loop, constantly moving towards the future but, thanks to the twist in space-time, circling back to revisit events in your own past. It's like having a personal time rollercoaster.

But, and it's a big but, achieving this cosmic feat would demand an astronomical amount of energy, perhaps on the scale of an exploding star. That's way beyond our current technological capabilities. Think of it like trying to power your house with a single AAA battery—it just won't cut it.

Yet, who knows? Maybe an advanced civilization out there, far more evolved than ours, has cracked the code. Imagine them zipping around in super-advanced vehicles, effortlessly navigating the twists and turns of time.

Now, let's bring Sergey Panamerenko back into the picture. Did he stumble upon this cosmic shortcut when he snapped that peculiar photograph? Could he have, intentionally or not, harnessed the secrets of time travel? While our current understanding might not have all the answers, the intrigue of Sergey's journey hints at the mysteries that lie at the intersection of theoretical physics and the boundless

PRABAL JAIN

possibilities of the cosmos.

◆ ◆ ◆

CHAPTER 3: EXPOSING THE TALE

Separating Fact from Fiction

Now that we've delved into the theoretical wonders of time travel, let's circle back to Sergey Panamerenko's mysterious journey. Could he have ventured into the cosmic unknown when he captured that peculiar UFO photograph? Did he slip through a wormhole or tear in the fabric of space-time? Let's untangle the threads of truth.

As we've journeyed through the story of Sergey Panamerenko, it's crucial to sift through fact and fiction. The idea of time travel, though theoretically possible, doesn't automatically validate every extraordinary tale. So, is this story of Sergey Panamerenko's time-traveling adventure true? Well, buckle up, because we're about to uncover the real story.

After tracking down the original full-length documentary and going through the painstaking process of translating it from Russian, a few red flags emerged. In the credits, there's a casting director listed, raising eyebrows about dramatized scenes. Furthermore, discrepancies within the story itself cast doubt on its authenticity.

For starters, the police officer in the documentary mentions Sergey's appearance on Tuesday, April 23, 2006. However, both the camera in the lobby and a basic calendar check reveal that date was a Sunday. Small but significant details like this raise questions about the accuracy of the narrative.

Digging deeper, during Sergey's first visit to the doctor, he claims to be born in June 1932, while his ID states March. Such inconsistencies contribute to a growing suspicion that the tale might be more fiction than fact.

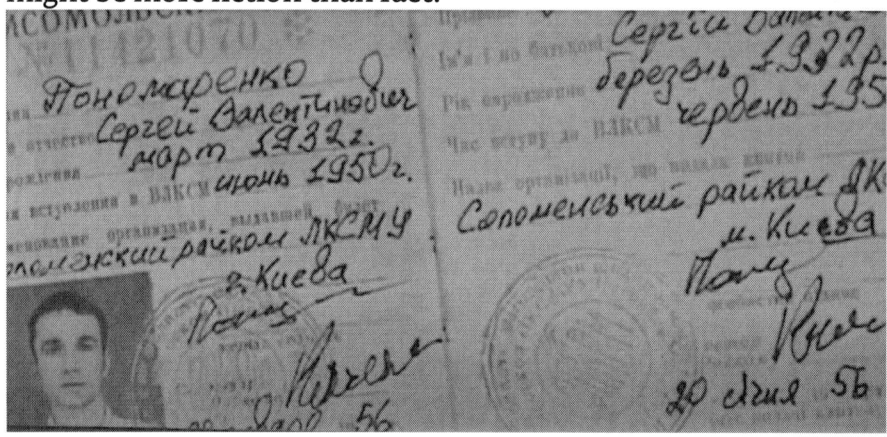

As we continue our exploration into Sergey Panamerenko's curious tale, the inconsistencies begin to cast doubt on the narrative's authenticity. During Sergey's second visit to the doctor, the timestamps on April 25th at 10:39 a.m. further muddy the waters, with dates and times appearing disjointed and incongruent.

Now, let's scrutinize the visual evidence. The missing person's report features a picture of Sergey with distinct clothing and a peculiar collar. Strikingly, when Sergey sends a picture to Valentina, the same attire and flipped collar make an appearance. While his expressions differ, digital aging attempts to bridge the gap. These oversights, including the identical collar, point to a meticulously crafted but flawed production.

In essence, while the storyline may captivate with its time-traveling allure, meticulous scrutiny reveals the fingerprints of fabrication. The actors' convincing portrayals and skillful use of visuals, when observed from a distance, create a captivating illusion. It's a testament to the power of storytelling, even when the threads of reality begin to unravel.

So, why does time travel hold such an irresistible allure? Perhaps it's because time is an omnipresent force, indifferent to wealth or power. Regardless of status, time claims us all. The concept of time travel sparks thoughts of the unknown future and the mysteries that may unfold after our time has passed. It also serves as a reminder of the limitations and impossibilities that accompany our existence.

While Sergey Panamerenko's tale turned out to be a carefully crafted fiction, it stands as a testament to the enduring fascination with time travel. It's a realm where imagination dances with the constraints of reality, offering a glimpse into the infinite possibilities that time, the enigmatic master of us all, might hold.

As we navigate the corridors of time, we confront not only the boundless possibilities of the future but also the echoes of the past—the decisions, mistakes, and regrets that shape our journey. How many moments in your life would you revisit if given the chance? Perhaps you'd silence that cringe-worthy comment in class, stand up to a childhood bully, or extend kindness to a fellow traveler on the bus.

It's easy to get lost in the labyrinth of "what-ifs," but here's a trick to reclaim a semblance of control over time. Whenever faced with a challenging decision, consider this: ten or twenty years from now, your future self will reflect on today. Regrets may surface, thoughts of alternative choices, paths not taken. So, in this moment, be kind to your future self.

Embrace the power of now by taking chances, extending kindness, and not letting the small stuff overshadow the grand tapestry of life. Your future self will thank you for the decisions made today. Time, the elusive currency of existence, is finite for all of us. Whether the journey concludes next year or half a century from now, you wouldn't want to gaze back with regret, whispering, "I should have" or "I wish I did."

So, as you journey through the inevitable passage of time, make each moment count. Be the architect of your time story. When the final chapter arrives, whether sooner or later, let your only thought be, "What a hell of a ride it was." Seize the present, shape your narrative, and let your journey through time be a testament to a life well-lived.

❖ ❖ ❖

PART 5: SAVIOR OF TOMORROW

John Titor's Time Traveling Mission

INTRODUCTION

In the riveting tale of "Chronicles of Tomorrow," we are thrust into a future that teeters on the brink of devastation. Imagine a United States torn apart by a second Civil War, a cataclysmic World War unleashing nuclear horrors, and a post-apocalyptic world where the remnants of humanity struggle amidst ruins, scarcity, and rampant disease. By 2038, a global blackout plunges civilization into a second Dark Age.

But amidst this chaos, hope emerges from an unexpected source – John Teeter, born in a small Florida town in 1998. Unbeknownst to him, he is destined to become a temporal soldier sent back in time on a mission to rewrite history and prevent this apocalyptic nightmare.

The story takes root in 1998 when, during an episode of Coast to Coast AM, hosted by Art Bell, a mysterious fax claiming to be from the future arrives. The fax, feeling eerily real, details the invention of time travel in 2034, using a Singularity engine. This engine allows for journeys both forward and backward in time, creating divergent timelines.

As we delve into the intricacies of time travel, we follow John Teeter's journey, discovering the profound implications of altering the past. The narrative unfolds with simplicity, mirroring the clarity of well-loved books, as it guides readers through the complexities of timelines, Singularity engines, and the quest to reshape a doomed future.

◆ ◆ ◆

CHAPTER 1: A GLIMPSE BEYOND

Time Traveler's Intricate Tapestry

In the world of temporal journeys as described by the mysterious fax, turning off the Singularity engine unveils a fresh timeline. The arrival of a time traveler, like John Teeter, and their machine in a different time creates a new reality, a divergent path from the original.

The narrative sheds light on the intriguing outcomes of time travel. One notable aspect is the possibility of encountering oneself in the newly formed timeline. John Teeter, the temporal soldier, has ventured into this self-discovery often, even taking along younger versions of himself for a few rides before returning to the altered timeline and going back to his own.

Moreover, the ability to alter history in the new universe is a powerful consequence. Changes can be subtle, like noticing unfamiliar car models or delayed book releases. The intricacies of these alterations become a central theme as the story unfolds, adding a layer of suspense to the time-travel narrative.

However, not all mysteries are easily unraveled. A significant revelation surfaces – time travelers heading forward from 2036 hit an inexplicable barrier in the year 2564. The plea for understanding and the call to pray for the discovery of this enigma hangs in the air, setting the stage for deeper exploration into the limitations of time travel.

As the narrative progresses, a second fax arrives, introducing another time traveler. This traveler, unlike the first, expresses a willingness to share information about the future, offering a glimpse into the intricacies of time, the physics behind time travel, and events yet to unfold. Art Bell, intrigued by the tantalizing prospect, awaits further revelations that could potentially unveil the secrets of a working time machine and the science that propels it.

Two years after the mysterious time traveler's faxes to Art Bell left listeners yearning for proof, their wish was granted. In a fascinating turn of events, a user named "Time Traveler Zero," later revealed to be John Teeter, emerged on the Time Travel Institute message board on November 2nd, 2000.

In his inaugural post, John Teeter introduced himself as a time traveler from the year 2036. His mission? Acquiring an IBM 5100 computer system from the year 1975. His time machine, described as a stationary Mass Temporal Displacement Unit manufactured by General Electric, was powered by two topspin dual-positive singularities, generating a standard offset Tipler sinusoid.

Skepticism loomed on the message board, as is expected when someone claims to be a time traveler. However, John Teeter's posts were remarkably specific, showcasing a depth of specialized knowledge. He delved into the theoretical method of time travel known as the Tipler sinusoid, outlined in a paper by Frank Tipler in 1974, setting the stage for an intriguing narrative.

The question of why a time traveler, equipped with advanced technology, would need a computer from 1975 added another layer of curiosity. John Teeter explained that the IBM 5100 was crucial for debugging legacy computer programs in 2036, addressing a potential problem with Unix in 2038. He drew a parallel with the Y2K scare, where concerns arose about hardware and software issues when the year changed from 99 to 00. While Y2K didn't bring about the doomsday scenarios some feared, it did cause sporadic problems. John Teeter warned of a similar issue in 2038 for Unix systems, providing a tangible link between past technological challenges and future pitfalls.

◆ ◆ ◆

CHAPTER 2: THE TIME TRAVELER'S WISDOM

As we delve deeper into John Teeter's revelations on the Time Travel Institute message board, the focus shifts to the Y2K scare and the impending challenge in 2038 concerning Unix systems. John Teeter, in his distinctive way, breaks down the complexities of Unix timestamps, elucidating that these systems measure time in seconds, with a timestamp being the count of seconds since January 1st, 1970.

The critical juncture lies in the limitations of 32-bit integers, capable of reaching only about 2.1 billion. With the official last date recognizable by a 32-bit system being Tuesday, January 19, 2038, John forewarns that things could become "interesting" after that point. Delving into the geeky details, he explains the necessity of upgrading systems to 64 bits, extending the timestamp capabilities to about 9.2 quintillion and securing us until the distant year 292 billion.

The narrative then circles back to the IBM 5100, connecting the dots between John Teeter's mission and the computer's unique capabilities. He asserts that the IBM 5100 could aid in debugging legacy code, citing its special functionality hidden from the public. While most personal computers of the time supported basic programming language, the 5100 had the rare ability to run APL programs designed for IBM mainframes, a well-kept secret known only to the IBM engineers who crafted it.

John Teeter's foresight gains credence as the narrative draws parallels with real-world instances, such as NASA resorting to eBay in 2002 to acquire Intel 8086 chips for missions. His initial post on the message board, laden with sound science and information not widely known at the time, positions him as a purveyor of wisdom and insight. Far from being a one-time revelation, John Teeter remains an active participant on the message board, generously engaging with questions and solidifying his role as a guide through the intricate realms of time travel.

Navigating Divergent Timelines

As John Teeter continued to share his insights on the message board, it became evident that he was just scratching the surface of his temporal wisdom. Actively engaging with the community, he willingly answered a multitude of questions, excluding only topics like the stock market or Super Bowl outcomes, emphasizing his disinterest in facilitating wealth accumulation.

Teeter acknowledged the limitations of his predictions, especially regarding events like sports outcomes, attributing potential inaccuracies to the concept of "divergence." In his analogy, he envisioned a cone representing the divergence between his timeline and the destination time. The farther back or forward in time one traveled, the larger the divergence. Upon arriving in the year 2000, Teeter noted a divergence of about one or two percent, enough to influence different outcomes, such as sports game results.

Teeter's explanation aligned with the many-worlds interpretation of quantum mechanics, where every possible outcome occurs in a separate timeline. Specifically referring to the Everett-Wheeler model, he showcased a commendable understanding of quantum mechanics, demonstrating his grasp of the scientific theories underpinning his time-travel narrative.

While Teeter refrained from making trivial predictions, he unfolded his own life and the future with remarkable detail. He foretold a tumultuous period in the early 2000s, foreseeing monthly Waco-type events that escalated into a Civil War in the United States by 2004. Joining a shotgun infantry unit named the "Fighting Diamondbacks" at the age of 13, John Teeter became a participant in this conflict that endured until 2015. The war culminated in what he termed a brief World War III, sparked by Russia's opportunistic attacks on cities in the United States, China, and Europe. The devastating retaliation resulted in the loss of three billion lives, painting a grim picture of the potential consequences of divergent timelines.

In the aftermath of the devastating World War III, which claimed the lives of nearly three billion people, the surviving population faced a drastically altered reality. Those who managed to escape the carnage were primarily individuals avoiding the big cities. The United States underwent a profound transformation, splintering into five distinct regions. Each region elected its president, collectively forming a significantly diminished federal government headquartered in Omaha, Nebraska, by 2036.

John Teeter, situated in Central Florida with his family, described a world reshaped by the war's aftermath. The surviving populace drew closer together, emphasizing the importance of family and community. Life became centered around personal connections, with people residing in proximity to their parents. The absence of large industrial complexes shifted the focus from mass production to local cultivation, creating a simpler and more sustainable existence. Reading, face-to-face conversations, and a renewed emphasis on religion became integral parts of daily life.

One prevalent concern in this new world was the global spread of mad cow disease, which had evolved into a pandemic. Amidst this transformed reality, John Teeter found himself part of a military unit comprising seven other time travelers. Their collective mission was to travel back in time, aiming to prevent as much environmental damage as possible.

Despite the detailed narrative John Teeter crafted, skepticism lingered among the message board community. Intrigued yet cautious, they sought more concrete evidence. Responding to their queries, John Teeter willingly provided diagrams of his time travel device, pictures of the operator's manual, and even images of the device itself. His openness extended to explaining that time travel was discovered in 2034 by scientists at CERN, grounding his narrative in a plausible scientific context.

While entertaining and fascinating, John Teeter's revelations left the audience intrigued and skeptical, prompting a dual desire for both understanding the mechanics of his time travel device and visual proof of its existence. In the subsequent sections, the narrative is poised to delve into the intricacies of time travel technology, offering readers a deeper understanding of John Teeter's extraordinary journey.

◆ ◆ ◆

CHAPTER 3: REVELATIONS OF TIME TRAVEL TECHNOLOGY

Delving into the intricacies of John Teeter's time travel technology, he shared comprehensive details on the breakthroughs that enabled General Electric to create functional time travel devices. According to him, the pivotal discovery occurred in 2034 when scientists at CERN unraveled the secrets of time travel.

General Electric's innovation resulted in various iterations and improvements in time travel devices. The specific unit John Teeter used was the C204 Gravity Distortion Time Displacement Unit. This machine operated using micro singularities or tiny black holes as a source of power. Two micro singularities, created, captured, and processed at a large circular facility, provided the gravitational manipulation needed for time travel. Electrons were injected under the surface of their respective urbispheres to control their mass, and the electricity required came from batteries.

One fascinating aspect of John Teeter's time machine involved "Cur black holes," which are rotating black holes linked to Tipler cylinders, aligning with real theories in physics that explore time travel concepts.

The heart of the time travel technology was the Variable Gravity Lock System (VGL). Since the machine solely traversed time and not space, the VGL ensured that the Earth maintained its position in orbit when reaching the destination, preventing the undesirable scenario of floating in space. The VGL, a system akin to the BGL (Variable Gravity Lock), played a crucial role in plotting the course and maintaining a consistent position in the environment during time travel.

The BGL system periodically checked and adjusted the field to ensure stability. If any variation occurred, the system could either reverse course or drop out of the time travel sequence. To avoid collisions with buildings and terrain features, sensors within the VGL continuously monitored the surroundings.

John Teeter's detailed explanations not only provided insights into the technology powering time travel but also showcased a deep understanding of the challenges and solutions associated with temporal journeys. The revelation of diagrams, operator's manuals, and device images added tangible elements to his narrative, inviting readers to explore the extraordinary world of time travel.

Navigating Time Travel Challenges

The intricacies of time travel continued to unfold as John Teeter elaborated on the operational aspects of the C204 Gravity Distortion Time Displacement Unit. The journey to the correct day relied on an array of computers, clocks, and sensors within the C204. The unit's ability to navigate and avoid unexpected obstacles, such as buildings and terrain features, showcased the sophistication of its technology. If the VGL sensors detected an unexpected mass in the target world line, the system would promptly shut down.

Addressing a question about traveling back a thousand years, John Teeter emphasized the limitations inherent in time travel.

As timelines diverge significantly the further backward or forward one goes, the C204's accuracy maxed out at around 60 years. Even in 2036, attempting to travel back a thousand years was deemed impractical due to the inherent error in the system. The divergence between the world line of origin and the target world line would be too substantial, resulting in a historical landscape unrecognizable to the time traveler.

The mechanics of reaching the target destination involved using gravity sensors and atomic clocks. With the second as the basic unit of calculation, the computer system controlled the distortion field at maximum power. However, John Teeter admitted that time travel, with the existing technology, was not an exact science. Inherent errors and chaos in the computer's calculations limited the accuracy of distortion units to approximately 60 years.

In a candid acknowledgment of the challenges, John Teeter explained that attempting to travel back a millennium would yield unpredictable results. Historical events would deviate significantly from expectations, making encounters with figures like Christ improbable. The divergence in the world line would create a reality where certain events never occurred.

❖ ❖ ❖

CHAPTER 4: THE PRACTICALITIES OF TIME TRAVEL

John Teeter's Departure

John Teeter's unconventional choice of a 1967 Chevy as the initial host for his time machine added a touch of familiarity to the extraordinary concept of time travel. Steering clear of the cliché DeLorean associated with time travel, he opted for vehicles that could accommodate the weight of the C204 Gravity Distortion Time Displacement Unit and navigate various terrains. The choice of a truck later on was motivated by the need for a robust suspension system capable of handling the C204's considerable weight.

The practicality of the vehicles was grounded in the fact that the time machine, being immobile in space, required physical transport to the desired location before initiating time travel. John's selection of inconspicuous vehicles aligned with his strategy of blending into the times he visited.

Addressing the curiosity about the sensation of time travel, John Teeter provided a vivid description. As the gravity field generated by the unit took over, travelers experienced a rapid and noticeable tug toward the unit, akin to the sensation of swiftly rising in an elevator. The intensity of this pull correlated with the power setting, with a maximum force of up to 2G. While there were no severe side effects, John recommended avoiding eating before a flight.

Contrary to cinematic depictions, there was no external bright flash of light during time travel. Instead, the vehicle appeared to accelerate, with light bending around it. To protect against a short burst of ultraviolet radiation, travelers had to wear sunglasses or close their eyes during this phase. John likened the visual experience to driving under a rainbow, followed by a fade to black until the time travel concluded.

Practical considerations extended to managing heat buildup outside the vehicle, prompting the advice to keep windows closed during time travel. The gravity field also created a small air pocket around the car, serving as the sole oxygen supply unless supplemental compressed air was brought along.

Amidst the skepticism surrounding his revelations, John Teeter remained steadfast in his mission, emphasizing that his goal wasn't necessarily to be believed. Despite the gravity of the war-related news he shared, he observed society's passive response, questioning why individuals allowed the erosion of their Constitution and the widespread suffering caused by poisoned food and uncaring indifference.

In a moment of candor, John hinted at a harsh future perspective, describing the present as full of lazy, self-centered, and civically ignorant individuals. He urged people to redirect their concern from him to the societal issues at hand.

John Teeter maintained a mysterious persona, never revealing his face or real name. One individual claimed a close relationship with him—Pamela Moore, an active participant on the message boards. Pamela and John engaged in numerous conversations over the internet. Before his departure, John promised Pamela a video as a farewell, providing her with a secret song to act as a password for verification. However, as of the latest update, the promised departure video had not materialized, and Pamela had not disclosed the secret song.

On March 24, 2001, John Teeter left a final message, signaling his imminent departure from the world line. Acknowledging that only a select few knew the exact timing of his exit, he expressed gratitude for the intriguing discussions in the last few days.

As John Teeter approached his departure, he acknowledged the handful of individuals privy to the exact timing, assuring that they would inform the community once he was gone. Expressing appreciation for the intriguing discussions in the final days, he delved into a thought-provoking reflection on the collective question about the absence of visible time travelers in the past.

From an objective viewpoint, John offered an expanded explanation, drawing on a personal experience. He recounted a highway journey with his parents, where they encountered distressed individuals with vehicle issues. Observing the reluctance of passersby to offer help, John revealed a parallel with the temporal drivers' hesitancy to reveal themselves in the past. The underlying reason, he explained, was fear—fear of the risks involved in intervening and fear that their efforts might go unappreciated or misunderstood.

Drawing a parallel to contemporary scenarios where people with car troubles might have cell phones or could walk to a gas station, John highlighted the perceived futility and risks of temporal intervention. He emphasized that the inherent risks and the belief that their assistance would likely be met with skepticism deterred time travelers from revealing themselves.

Despite acknowledging Pamela for her assistance with emails and expressing gratitude for the intelligent and insightful questions from others, John reiterated his parting thought. Reflecting on a recurring theme, he clarified that he did not have a secret agenda. However, he had closely observed the world line, framing his interaction as a secondary mission protocol based on standing orders for all temporal drivers.

The secondary objective, he explained, was not a direct mission parameter but rather an indirect engagement with the world line's inhabitants. John's farewell carried an air of caution and a glimpse into the complexities of temporal missions, where the balance between observation and intervention posed inherent challenges and risks that time travelers were cautious to navigate.

❖ ❖ ❖

CHAPTER 5: THE LEGACY UNFOLDS

Exposing John Teeter's Predictions

As the legend of John Teeter unfolded, it became clear that his story didn't end with his departure in 2001. Over the years, the accuracy of his predictions became a subject of scrutiny. While some prophecies didn't materialize, others seemed to echo current events.

One notable prediction was a Civil War in the United States, foreseen for 2005. While this prediction didn't come to pass, the observation was made that America has arguably never been more divided, reflecting the polarization seen in contemporary society. Additionally, John Teeter foresaw a nuclear war in 2015, which didn't occur, but the current global climate suggests an ongoing threat.

Not all predictions missed the mark; John accurately foresaw a mad cow disease outbreak in the early 2000s. This prediction aligned with America's first confirmed case of bovine spongiform encephalitis (BSE) in six years, emphasizing the potential dangers associated with such infections.

As John Teeter posted in 2001, the majority accessed the internet through dial-up modems. He predicted a future where the internet would undergo significant changes, a forecast that aligns with the evolution of the digital landscape over the years.

While some aspects of John Teeter's predictions proved inaccurate, the ongoing societal relevance and occasional alignment with real-world events have perpetuated the legend, leaving room for continued speculation and fascination with the enigmatic time traveler's tale.

As of John Teeter's last posts in 2001, the internet landscape was dominated by dial-up modems. In a foresight that aligns with today's reality, John predicted a future where the internet would resemble the current cell phone system. His vision of a decentralized entertainment industry, where anyone could create and share videos, mirrors the rise of platforms like YouTube that have surpassed traditional networks and cinemas in audience engagement.

John Teeter's clairvoyance extended to the realm of high-energy physics at CERN, as he predicted breakthroughs in 2013, notably the confirmation of the Higgs boson. Additionally, he challenged Stephen Hawking's initial belief that everything entering a black hole vanishes forever, a claim later revised by Hawking.

While some may attribute these predictions to an informed individual making educated guesses, the story isn't without its skeptics. Critics point to inconsistencies and convenient coincidences within the narrative, raising doubts about the authenticity of John Teeter's time-travel claims. The assertion that his predictions might have come true in alternate timelines, as proposed by adherents of the many-worlds theory, remains unverifiable.

Despite the intriguing aspects of John Teeter's story, some argue that it might be a carefully crafted hoax. In the pursuit of uncovering the true identity behind John Teeter, a few names consistently emerge. Joseph Matheny, a writer and transmedia artist known for his involvement in alternate reality games like "Ong's Hat," is often considered a prime suspect. Matheny himself has claimed involvement in developing the John Teeter story as a playful endeavor with three collaborators.

The mystery surrounding John Teeter's identity and the authenticity of his time-travel account continues to captivate minds, prompting a blend of fascination, skepticism, and a quest for the truth behind this enigmatic tale.

Joseph Matheny, widely recognized for his involvement in one of the pioneering alternate reality games, "Ong's Hat," emerges as a key figure in the potential creation of the John Teeter story. Notably, "Ong's Hat" was among the earliest instances of alternate reality or real-time interactive games. Matheny asserts that he, along with three other collaborators, developed the John Teeter narrative as a lighthearted experiment to create an internet myth, and he claims success in this endeavor.

Matheny refuses to disclose the identities of his co-conspirators, citing their prominent positions in the entertainment industry and the need to protect their reputations. According to Matheny, the time machine depicted in the fuzzy photos was crafted by a professional prop designer with experience in major films. Enthusiastic John Teeter followers have reportedly identified components of the time machine as real-world objects.

One of Matheny's explanations for the varying tones in the messages attributed to John Teeter is that they were composed by different individuals within the team. Matheny himself takes credit for character development, and he acknowledges that the similarities between John Teeter's story and that of John Connor were intentional.

Initially skeptical of Matheny's technical and scientific acumen, considering his background in the entertainment industry, it turns out Matheny has a substantial tech background. He has been involved in the tech scene since the 80s, collaborating with companies like Adobe and Netscape, and holds patents. His game, "Ong's Hat," even incorporated references to theoretical physics, showcasing his ability to blend technology and storytelling.

While Matheny doesn't provide concrete evidence of his involvement in the John Teeter narrative, his annoyance at persistent inquiries suggests a weariness with the ongoing speculation. Despite his assertion that people can choose to believe him or not, the quest for the truth behind John Teeter's tale persists, with other potential creators in the spotlight, including Larry Haber and the Haber Brothers.

◆ ◆ ◆

CHAPTER 6: LARRY HABER'S ROLE IN THE JOHN TEETER STORY

A Lawyer's Unusual Connection

Larry Haber, a Florida-based entertainment attorney, steps into the spotlight in the John Teeter narrative, claiming to represent John Teeter's mom, known as K, and the Teeter family. While Larry might not possess the technical or scientific background typically associated with creating a complex tale like John Teeter's, his brothers, Richard Haber, an I.T administrator, and Maury Haber, a senior cybersecurity professional, bring a different set of skills to the table.

In interviews with Larry Haber, it becomes evident that he lacks the technological expertise required to craft the intricate details found in John Teeter's story. However, his brothers, especially Maury Haber, have the technical know-how and experience in cybersecurity and technology. Maury also has a history of writing about technology, adding another layer to the potential collaboration.

Enter John Rasmus Houston, the investigator behind the YouTube channel "Hoax Hunter." Houston delves deep into the John Teeter saga, conducting exhaustive research that includes tracking P.O. boxes, comparing writing styles between Maury Haber and John Teeter, and examining usernames from the message board. Houston's conclusion points towards Maury

Haber being the likely identity behind John Teeter, with Larry Haber eventually joining the story to represent it legally.

Larry Haber's connection to John Teeter goes beyond legal representation. In 2003, he registered the John Teeter Foundation LLC, a for-profit business responsible for publishing John Teeter's posts in book form titled "A Time Traveler's Tale." Additionally, Larry registered "John Teeter" as a trademark in 2007, indicating a level of commercialization associated with the story.

Larry Haber's role in the John Teeter saga raises eyebrows as he simultaneously claims to represent the Teeter family and engages in businesses and books profiting from the narrative. This apparent conflict of interest prompts scrutiny, and while Larry Haber does not confirm Joseph Matheny's claim that Matheny influenced the removal of his book from publication, the book is confirmed to be out of print.

Despite potential conflicts, Larry Haber seems unfazed. His jokes about lawyers add a touch of humor, and he maintains a pragmatic stance, asserting that he's simply working for his client and earning a living. Even Pamela Morris, who received a copy of Larry Haber's book signed by John, doesn't disclose the secret song supposedly included.

In Larry Haber's defense, he maintains a neutral stance on the believability of the John Teeter story. He states that he doesn't know whether the story is true or false and expresses a lack of concern, emphasizing his professional commitment to his client.

The enduring allure of the John Teeter story lies in its ability to captivate imaginations and spark discussions about possibilities and choices. Time travel narratives, especially those depicting ominous futures, prompt reflection on our present circumstances and offer the chance to alter our trajectory. The desire for guidance from someone who has witnessed such a future persists, with John Teeter's warnings about avoiding certain products serving as a thought-provoking aspect of the narrative.

As we navigate the complexities of the John Teeter story, questions linger about its true origins, the involvement of various individuals, and the interplay between legal representation and commercial ventures. The tale continues to fascinate, resonating with our collective fascination for time travel and its potential impact on our lives.

◆ ◆ ◆

CHAPTER 7: JOHN TEETER'S SURVIVAL ADVICE AND PERSONAL PREPAREDNESS

Before John Teeter vanished, he left behind survival advice that, whether rooted in fact or fiction, has prompted some to take precautions. His recommendations include:

1. Dietary Choices:

   - Avoid consuming products from animals that are fed parts of their own deceased counterparts.

2. Intimate Relations:

   - Refrain from intimate relations or kissing with individuals whose background is unfamiliar to you.

3. Basic Sanitation and Water Purification:

   - Acquire knowledge about basic sanitation practices and water purification methods.

4. Firearm Familiarity:

   - Develop comfort and proficiency with firearms, including learning to shoot and clean a gun.

5. First Aid Skills:

   - Obtain a quality first aid kit and learn how to use it effectively.

6. Building Trust Networks:

- Identify and establish trust with five individuals within a 100-mile radius, maintaining regular contact with them.

7. Understanding the U.S. Constitution:

- Read and familiarize yourself with the U.S. Constitution.

8. Physical Preparedness:

- Own a bicycle with two sets of spare tires and ride it for at least 10 miles per week.

9. Evacuation Preparedness:

- Consider what items you would take if you had only 10 minutes to leave your home permanently.

While the authenticity of John Teeter's story remains uncertain, some individuals, like the narrator's family, have chosen to heed his advice. They have taken practical steps to prepare for a future that aligns with the cautionary tale John shared. Whether you believe in John Teeter's time-travel narrative or not, the decision to follow or dismiss his guidance ultimately rests on personal choice and risk tolerance.

◆ ◆ ◆

PART 6: THE MONTAUK PROJECT

The Philadelphia Experiment

INTRODUCTION

The Enigma of the USS Eldridge

In 1943, something extraordinary happened to the USS Eldridge—a naval ship vanished from the waters of Philadelphia and reappeared in Virginia. This mysterious event, now known as the Philadelphia Experiment, captured the imagination of many. When the Eldridge reemerged, some crew members faced a horrifying fate: they materialized within walls and bulkheads, leading to their agonizing demise. Strangely, two sailors, brothers by chance, didn't return at all. Presumed dead or lost, they had, in fact, traveled 40 years into the future.

Their destination? A covert military base on the east end of Long Island, part of a secret project known as Montauk. Fast forward to the early '70s, where Preston Nichols, an engineer specializing in electromagnetism, worked on Long Island for a defense contractor. During this time, Nichols delved into the realms of telepathy with a group of psychics, achieving remarkable results.

However, a puzzling pattern emerged. Like clockwork, every day at the same time, the psychics' minds were inexplicably blocked. After three years of grappling with this enigma, Nichols decided to investigate further. Armed with radio equipment, he discovered that the mysterious signal blocking telepathic abilities occurred when the frequency 410 to 420 megahertz was detected.

Nichols, driven by curiosity, crafted a mobile transceiver to trace the origin of this signal. To his astonishment, the signal led him to Montauk Point on the east end of Long Island, New York. This revelation marked the beginning of an intriguing journey into the heart of the Montauk Project, where the fabric of time and reality seemed to intertwine.

Join us as we unravel the secrets of the USS Eldridge, the Philadelphia Experiment, and the mysterious events that unfolded at Montauk Point—a journey through time that challenges our understanding of the world we live in.

◆ ◆ ◆

CHAPTER 1: THE MYSTERIES OF MONTAUK

After tracing the mysterious signal to a large radar tower on Montauk Air Force Base, Preston Nichols found himself at a crossroads. The radio interference persisted for years, only to cease without explanation. Life moved on, and Nichols didn't give it much thought until a friend's call revealed that the air force base was now abandoned, urging him to investigate.

Upon arrival, Nichols discovered a scene contrary to what one would expect from a decommissioned military base. Montauk Air Force Base was deserted but in disarray, as if abandoned in haste. Nichols, driven by curiosity, ventured further and stumbled upon a young homeless man taking refuge in one of the deserted buildings. The man, claiming to be a military technician, disclosed a shocking revelation—the base was abandoned due to the appearance of a colossal beast that wreaked havoc, leading to the abrupt shutdown of a project.

Perplexed by this revelation, Nichols probed further, seeking clarity on the terms "beast" and "project." The young man seemed equally bewildered and dropped a bombshell: "You don't remember? You're Preston Nichols. You ran the Montauk Project."

In 1984, Nichols joined forces with a gifted psychic named Duncan Cameron. Duncan's arrival at the abandoned base was nothing short of astonishing—he navigated the grounds with uncanny familiarity, recognizing buildings and recalling specific details like the location of the mess hall. As they delved deeper into the mysteries of Montauk, Duncan began unraveling a series of disturbing experiments that unfolded on the property over the years.

It became apparent that Duncan was not merely an observer but an unwitting participant in these experiments. The duo's exploration led them to the imposing transmitter building, where Duncan's demeanor took an unexpected turn. The secrets of the Montauk Project awaited revelation as Duncan delved into memories buried in the shadows of time.

As Duncan Cameron and Preston Nichols continued their exploration of the Montauk Project, a startling revelation unfolded within the walls of the large transmitter building. Duncan, entering a trance-like state, confessed that he had been programmed to find Nichols, befriend him, and ultimately, carry out a dark mission—to kill Nichols and obliterate his lab along with all its research.

Awareness of this sinister programming empowered Duncan to resist its commands. Back at Nichols' lab, a deprogramming technique was employed, restoring full control of Duncan's consciousness. This transformative experience prompted Nichols to confront his own involvement with the Montauk Project, even though the specifics remained elusive.

As Nichols and Duncan collaborated, more memories emerged from the shadows of Duncan Cameron's mind. Astonishingly, he realized that he and his brother Edward had served aboard the USS Eldridge and were the two sailors lost during the Philadelphia Experiment. The temporal anomaly that transported them from 1943 to 1983 unveiled a new layer of the enigmatic connection between the past and the present.

PRABAL JAIN

◆ ◆ ◆

CHAPTER 2: DUAL REALITIES UNVEILED

Paradigm Shifts and Mind Control

Preston Nichols' perplexing encounters with unexplained wounds took a disconcerting turn as the occurrences multiplied. On more than one occasion, he discovered fresh wounds covered by band-aids on his hand, wounds that seemingly appeared out of nowhere within a mere 15-minute span. Frustrated and confused, Nichols even sought clarification from the company nurse, who had no record of him seeking band-aid assistance.

As time passed, Nichols found himself entangled in what he could only describe as living two separate lives. A peculiar intuition led him to a high-security area—the basement. Despite lacking the necessary clearance, he ventured down, assuming a natural demeanor. To his surprise, the security guard not only allowed him access but handed him a badge with his name on it, ushering him into an unfamiliar yet plush office.

There, on the large desk, sat a nameplate that bore a title shrouded in mystery: Preston B. Nichols, Assistant Project Director. This physical evidence shattered any doubt—Nichols was living a dual existence, one as an engineer and the other as a senior member of a clandestine government initiative known as the Montauk Project.

By early 1990, the fragments of Nichols' memories coalesced into a disturbing revelation. The Montauk Project, once buried in the recesses of his consciousness, resurfaced with unprecedented clarity. The magnitude of his involvement and the nature of the experiments conducted within the shadows of Montauk left Nichols grappling with a reality more unsettling than he could have fathomed.

Meanwhile, about 50 years after the Philadelphia Experiment, a man named Al Bielek began experiencing glimpses, visions, and entire memories of the life of Edward Cameron. As a young naval officer serving aboard the Eldridge with his brother Duncan, the echoes of the past intertwined with the present, creating a tapestry of enigma that spanned decades. The threads of these intertwined destinies would soon unravel, revealing deeper layers of the mysteries that bound these individuals across time and space.

As Al Bielek, aka Edward Cameron, began to experience vivid recollections of his life as a young naval officer aboard the USS Eldridge with his brother Duncan Cameron, the threads of time and destiny became intricately woven. Indeed, Duncan Cameron was the psychic collaborator working with Preston Nichols, 40 years in the future.

Al Bielek, fueled by his memories, became a prolific author, conference speaker, and interviewee. He shared his accounts of life on the USS Eldridge, particularly during the activation of what was termed a "magnetic bottle." As this magnetic force engaged, the ship started slipping through time. In a moment of panic, both Al Bielek (Edward Cameron) and Duncan jumped ship and found themselves in the year 2137.

Upon waking up in a hospital, Edward (Al Bielek) underwent treatment for radiation injuries. However, Duncan was nowhere to be found. As Edward's health improved, he delved into the unfamiliar world of 2137. The United States had undergone drastic geographical transformations—Florida and most of the Eastern Seaboard were submerged, California had become a series of islands, and the Great Lakes had merged into one vast lake.

The aftermath of a devastating nuclear war between the West, Russia, and China had reduced the global population to a mere 300 million. Governments, including the United States and Canada, had crumbled, leaving regions under local martial law. Just as Edward was grappling with these overwhelming changes, he found himself transported hundreds of years further into the future, landing in the year 2749.

In this distant era, life had evolved significantly. Anti-gravity technology had become commonplace, reshaping the way people lived. The two years Edward spent in the 28th century were marked by experiences and advancements beyond anything he could have imagined, providing a glimpse into a future vastly different from the 22nd century. The tale of Edward's journey through time continued to unfold, revealing the profound impact of temporal shifts on his understanding of the world and his place within it.

As Edward Cameron navigated life in the distant year of 2749, marked by floating cities suspended more than two miles above the Earth, the most striking change was the integration of anti-gravity technology. These ethereal cities were managed by an advanced artificial intelligence (AI), intricately interconnected to ensure seamless functioning. In this seemingly utopian future, human life was comfortable, provided one contributed to society. All needs were effortlessly met, with AI-operated robotic equipment handling farming and food production—an almost idyllic, communist-like paradise.

However, Edward couldn't shake the feeling that in this

seemingly perfect world, people had lost their individuality. Life may have been easier, but a sense of mindless conformity prevailed. It was a paradise of sorts, yet Edward questioned the cost of such comfort and the sacrifice of personal identity—a sentiment far removed from the envisioned utopia.

Suddenly, the trajectory of Edward's existence took another unexpected turn. He and his brother Duncan found themselves back in 1983, briefed by government officials with stern warnings never to disclose the events they had experienced. Now, Edward, under the alias Al Bielek, was embarking on what would be his most crucial mission yet.

In 1990, Duncan Cameron fully recollected the harrowing details of the Philadelphia Experiment and the Montauk Project. This revelation extended to Preston Nichols as well, and the memories they unearthed were nothing short of terrifying. Their journey through time and the perils of teleportation had captured the attention of researchers at Brookhaven National Labs in 1967. Technicians at Brookhaven made a groundbreaking discovery—the men aboard the USS Eldridge were susceptible to mind control.

This discovery held immense military potential. The United States could wield this technology to influence enemy armies, preventing wars and potentially dominating the planet without a single life lost. The implications of mind control on a global scale began to unfold, setting the stage for a chilling revelation of the dark underbelly of the experiments conducted under the guise of time travel and teleportation.

◆ ◆ ◆

CHAPTER 3: THE MONTAUK EXPERIMENT

Power of the Experiment

The prospect of controlling the minds of an enemy's army, paving the way for bloodless victories and global dominance, sent shivers down the spine. Yet, as the conversation turned to the present, skepticism surfaced—a notion that the government already exerted influence through news media, big tech, and Hollywood, steering public perception. The distinction between having a point of view and true mind control was debated, challenging the perceived boundary between manipulation and independent thought.

Returning to the Montauk Project, scientists from Brookhaven eagerly embarked on their endeavors at the Montauk Air Force Station—a secluded, deserted location, equipped with the necessary tools, including the world's largest radar antenna. This potent antenna could broadcast high-powered signals across vast distances. The objective was clear: to discover the right frequency capable of altering and controlling the human mind.

Duncan Cameron, with his exceptional psychic abilities, played a pivotal role in the project. His capacity to endure significant electromagnetic energy was crucial for surviving the Montauk Chair—a mind-reading device that became the epicenter of the experiment. The Montauk Chair, a formidable structure covered in coils and sensors, was linked to three receivers, six channels, and a Cray supercomputer. When an individual sat in the chair, their psychic abilities were exponentially amplified, projecting the images from their mind onto the computer screen.

The initial tests focused on the effects of electrocution with varying amounts and frequencies of energy on Cameron. These experiments revealed that different frequencies could evoke diverse emotions, and specific frequencies had the power to induce sleep—an intriguing avenue for potential manipulation. Notably, the transmissions also affected animals in the vicinity, hinting at the broader impact of the experiment on the environment.

The Montauk Experiment continued to push boundaries as researchers discovered that different frequencies could evoke various emotions, and specific frequencies had the ability to induce sleep. Beyond the confines of the laboratory, the effects extended to the local wildlife. Reports emerged of deer fleeing the woods, hurling themselves against storefront windows on Main Street—a bizarre manifestation of the experiment's influence.

Researchers, propelled by the unique psychic abilities of Duncan Cameron and the technological advancements at Montauk, achieved a significant milestone—the development of the "Seeing Eye." With a lock of someone's hair or a personal item, Cameron could see through that person's eyes, hear through their ears, and feel their bodily sensations, extending this connection globally, akin to the capabilities of remote viewers.

The experimentation took a darker turn as scientists delved into controlling people's thoughts. They mastered the technique of loading information, commands, and entire programs into an individual's mind, tailoring these manipulations to compel actions that individuals wouldn't naturally undertake—

assassination, sabotage, and even self-sacrifice if it aligned with the mission.

Advancements in the experiments reached new heights as Cameron manifested physical objects with his mind. Whether an apple or a baseball, the object would materialize first on the computer screen, then holographically, and finally as an actual, tangible object in the real world. This breakthrough set the stage for the Montauk Project's main experiment—an ambitious endeavor involving a colossal new antenna and multiple transmitters.

The goal? To create a vortex—a portal that someone could step through, transcending time itself. Dr. John von Neumann, a polymath with contributions to mathematics, physics, computer science, economics, and quantum mechanics, played a key role in this ambitious venture. The convergence of psychic abilities, cutting-edge technology, and the enigmatic vortex would thrust the Montauk Project into uncharted territory, challenging the very fabric of reality itself.

Dr. John von Neumann, renowned for his contributions to mathematics, physics, computer science, and more, played a pivotal role in top-secret government programs, including the Manhattan Project. Despite officially reported as having succumbed to cancer in 1958, Preston Nichols uncovered a startling truth—von Neumann had been placed in a program akin to witness protection, concealing his identity.

In a momentous meeting, Nichols engaged in a conversation with von Neumann, unveiling the intricate connections between the Montauk experiments and the Philadelphia Experiment. Von Neumann, now an elderly man, had been anticipating this reunion for 40 years. He disclosed a crucial revelation—when the USS Eldridge reappeared after the

Philadelphia Experiment, a malfunctioning power generator led to the tragic loss of many lives.

Von Neumann, armed with a solution, explained that disabling the faulty generator during the experiment's initial run would ensure the ship's proper return without casualties. Al Bielek and Duncan Cameron, selected for this vital mission, harbored understandable nerves. However, von Neumann reassured them, asserting his confidence in the success of their endeavor. According to the ship's records in Montauk, they had already accomplished this feat.

Duncan, sitting in the Montauk Chair, opened a portal to the USS Eldridge in 1943. Alongside his brother Edward, they leaped back to the ship and disabled the malfunctioning generator. Edward, opting to remain in 1943, initiated a pivotal change in the course of events. However, upon Duncan's return to Montauk, a mysterious twist awaited him—his multiple jumps through time had accelerated his aging process, leaving him on the brink of death from old age.

This unexpected turn of events introduced a new layer of complexity to the experiment's consequences, altering the fates of those involved in ways that transcended the bounds of the initial mission. The unraveling tale of the USS Eldridge, the Philadelphia Experiment, and the Montauk Project delved deeper into the enigma of time manipulation and its profound impact on the individuals entangled in its web.

◆ ◆ ◆

CHAPTER 4: NIGHTMARES AND CONTINGENCIES

The consequences of Duncan Cameron's accelerated aging, a result of his multiple time jumps, posed a dire threat. Rapidly aging and on the brink of death, Duncan's pivotal role in past events risked triggering paradoxes that could lead to disastrous consequences. To avert this potential catastrophe, Montauk technology was employed to send a message through time to Duncan's father, Duncan Cameron Senior.

At that time, Duncan Senior only had a daughter, but he received instructions to father baby boys as much depended on it. In 1951, Duncan Jr. was born, and Montauk scientists utilized the boy as a vessel for Duncan's current electromagnetic signature. This strategic move aimed to ensure the continuity of the timeline without creating paradoxes. In a parallel maneuver, employing age regression, Edward Cameron's consciousness was installed into the body of young Al Bielek, further complicating the intricate web of timelines.

Amidst these convoluted machinations, Preston Nichols, burdened by the weight of paradoxes and the potential harm wrought upon individuals and the fabric of spacetime, reached a critical decision. He determined it was time to shut down the Montauk Project. Unbeknownst to him, the project had a contingency protocol in place.

In a surreal moment, someone quietly approached Duncan while he was in the chair and whispered the cryptic phrase, "The time is now." This triggered a nightmarish event as Duncan, upon hearing those words, unleashed a monstrous entity from his subconscious. However, this creature didn't manifest within the confines of the lab; instead, it wreaked havoc somewhere on the Montauk base.

Preston Nichols vividly described the creature as at least 10 feet tall, hairy, and vicious, tearing through the base and attacking everything in its path. In a desperate attempt to contain the chaos, Nichols' supervisor ordered the shutdown of the power generators, but this drastic measure had consequences yet to unfold—a harrowing chapter in the Montauk Project's mysterious narrative.

The unleashed creature, a monstrous entity standing at least 10 feet tall, wreaked havoc on the Montauk base, defying attempts to contain it. Despite the shutdown of the Montauk transmitter, the creature continued its rampage unabated. Efforts to cut off its power source proved futile—the creature persisted, attacking buildings and instigating chaos.

In a desperate bid to quell the terror, Preston Nichols, armed with an acetylene torch, ventured to the building housing the transmitter control unit. Despite yanking out wires and attempting to sever connections, the creature showed no signs of relenting. The main power supply from the utility company was cut, yet power persisted from an unknown source. The creature's rampage continued, casting a shadow of dread over the Montauk base.

Nichols, undeterred, escalated his efforts. He dismantled the transmitter itself, cutting wires, conduits, and destroying large pieces of equipment in a desperate attempt to halt the nightmare. The building plunged into darkness, but the transmitter inexplicably continued to function. Distant screams echoed from somewhere on the base, heightening the sense of horror.

As Nichols persistently applied the acetylene torch to the transmitter, a pivotal moment unfolded—the portal created by Duncan Cameron closed, and the creature vanished. For Preston Nichols, this marked the conclusion of the Montauk Project, but for many victims entangled in this nightmarish experiment, it was merely the beginning.

The capacity to manipulate time, often deemed far-fetched, became a chilling reality in the late 1940s and early '50s. The Montauk Project, running from the early '70s to 1983, might seem incredulous, yet numerous individuals assert that Preston Nichols is recounting the truth. During its operation, the project required a constant supply of people for its experiments—an unfortunate reality that unfolded amidst the shadows of secrecy and temporal manipulation.

The Dark Chapter of the Montauk Boys

While the veracity of Preston Nichols' account remains a topic of debate, there is a haunting truth underlying the Montauk Project—the need for a constant supply of individuals for its experiments. Regrettably, a significant portion of these subjects were children, often boys aged between 10 and 15, who became known as the "Montauk Boys."

These boys, typically runaways or taken from troubled homes marked by issues like alcoholism, drug addiction, or abuse, became unwitting participants in a nightmarish chapter of covert experiments. One such individual, Stuart Swerdlow, a Montauk Boy, recollects haunting dreams of waking up in a dark, damp room, strapped to a hospital bed surrounded by strangers. According to Preston Nichols, these experiments unfolded deep beneath the Montauk Air Force Base.

A disturbing objective of the Montauk Project was to mold an army of programmable and controllable children. The idea was to activate them at any time, deploying them on missions, regardless of how horrific, and erase all memory of their actions. The Montauk Boys, tragically, have been linked to notorious events such as the Columbine shooting and the Oklahoma City bombing.

The process of programming these young minds was harrowing. Children underwent a systematic breakdown that involved starvation, torture, electric shocks, and near-drowning through submersion in cold water. This relentless conditioning continued until the child's mind was deemed ready to accept new programming. Numerous men have come forward, claiming to be Montauk Boys. Their testimonies include forced ingestion of LSD in what became known as the "acid house" and being used as human generators to feed psychics, often Duncan Cameron, sitting in the Montauk Chair.

As expected, many of these children did not emerge unscathed, bearing the lifelong scars of the horrors inflicted upon them in the name of clandestine experimentation. The dark legacy of the Montauk Boys casts a somber shadow on the covert activities that unfolded beneath the surface of the Montauk Project.

◆ ◆ ◆

CHAPTER 5: SHADOWS AND ANOMALIES

The torment inflicted on the Montauk Boys reached a grim pinnacle, with some accounts revealing the appalling use of a young boy's body as a kind of generator to feed psychics seated in the Montauk Chair—often Duncan Cameron. Tragically, many children did not survive this nightmarish phase of the experiment, their fates shrouded in mystery as they remain presumed missing even after four decades.

The sinister objectives of the Montauk Project extended to a desire for a substantial number of programmable boys, intended for deployment in mind control operations. The far-reaching impact of the experiments reached beyond the confines of the base, disrupting television and radio signals while causing erratic behavior in animals.

In 2008, an eerie discovery added to the mystique of Montauk —a creature known as the "Montauk Monster" washed up on the beach. This enigmatic being sparked speculation and raised questions about its origin. Directly across the Long Island Sound lies Plum Island, housing the Animal Disease Center. Rumors swirl around Plum Island, suggesting its involvement in animal experiments, biological weapons research, and even the testing of human-animal hybrids. Could the Montauk Monster have emerged from Plum Island, entwining the mysteries of these neighboring locations?

The intrigue deepens as we explore Christopher Garritano's

experiences. In 1983, at the tender age of eight, while playing on Montauk Beach, Garritano unearthed peculiar metal objects from the sand. His innocent curiosity quickly transformed into a chilling encounter when an individual in military uniform materialized out of nowhere, chasing him away from the beach. This encounter ignited a lifelong obsession for Garritano, leading him to revisit the base multiple times. Throughout these visits, he uncovered discrepancies in the government's official narrative, adding yet more layers to the enigma of Montauk.

Christopher Garritano's persistent visits to the Montauk Air Force Base unearthed unsettling discrepancies in the official narrative. Contrary to the government's assertions, the base, by design, is not meant to have underground levels. Garritano observed numerous manhole covers across the property, ostensibly for drainage purposes. However, a significant revelation occurred when Garritano, accompanied by a geophysicist, employed imaging equipment, confirming the existence of a large concrete building buried 20 feet below ground.

Further explorations conducted by various individuals over the years have yielded evidence of an underground complex, concealed and filled with concrete. Urban explorer Brian Minnick stumbled upon receipts from the late 1980s during one visit, revealing staggering expenditures of over $80,000 per week on food. This substantial financial outlay raises questions about the activities on a base supposedly shut down in 1981.

The roster of individuals claiming involvement in the same experiment extends beyond Garritano and includes Preston Nichols, Stewart Swerdlow, Al Bielek, and Brian Minnick, among others. Dozens of people share parallel narratives, all of which are vehemently denied by the U.S. government.

Amidst the conflicting accounts, a survivor of alleged government experiments, who identifies as a subject of radiation, mind control, and drug experiments, steps forward. This survivor, recalling the years 1966 to 1973, refers to a figure known as "Dr. Green" and denounces the actions of the United States government as shameful. The survivor, having endured a harrowing past, stands as a testament to the suffering inflicted upon those ensnared in clandestine experiments—knowledge that their families will carry with them for generations.

As the revelations unfold, the line between truth and denial becomes increasingly blurred, leaving individuals to grapple with the unsettling reality of covert government activities and the lasting impact on those who claim to be survivors of the Montauk Project.

Personal Horrors

The survivor of alleged government experiments bravely shares a deeply unsettling account of their ordeal. Identified as a mind control subject under the influence of someone known as "Dr. Green" from 1966 to 1973, the survivor condemns the actions of the United States government as shameful. Dr. Greene's primary objective was to gain control of their mind and train them to become a spy assassin.

The survivor reveals a particularly harrowing chapter in their experience, recounting a disturbing episode in 1967. Sent to a lodge in Maryland called Deep Creek Cabins, they were coerced into learning how to sexually please men, with the explicit purpose of extracting information. This traumatic training aimed to manipulate individuals into divulging personal details. The survivor expresses remorse for their involvement in these activities, acknowledging that the past cannot be undone.

The weight of this revelation extends beyond personal narratives. The survivor implores the power of forgiveness, recognizing the profound impact of their actions. The disclosure of such deeply personal and distressing experiences sheds light on the dark underbelly of covert government experiments.

Transitioning to the broader context of the Montauk Project, He shares a personal connection to the conspiracy, having spent much of their life on Long Island. The air force base, now named Camp Hero, holds a significant place in the conspiracy's lore. Notably, the original title of the popular TV show "Stranger Things" was "Montauk," drawing inspiration from Preston Nichols' writings.

However, this confronts the disconcerting reality that the more they delve into their favorite conspiracy theory, the less they appreciate the individuals involved. Casting doubt on the credibility of Al Bielek, who claimed to have served on the USS Eldridge in 1943 in the body of Edward Cameron, highlights the absence of any records supporting Bielek's account. Skepticism arises as supporters argue that the government erased or changed their names. Yet, he points out discrepancies, such as the use of pictures in Bielek's writings, raising questions about the authenticity of the claims.

◆ ◆ ◆

CHAPTER 6: EXPOSING CREDIBILITY

The narrative takes a critical turn as it examines the credibility of key figures in the Montauk Project saga. Al Bielek, a central character in the conspiracy, claimed to have served on the USS Eldridge in 1943, inhabiting the body of Edward Cameron. However, doubts arise as there are no records supporting Bielek's account. Suspicion deepens when it is revealed that pictures of his family, including Edward and Duncan Cameron, used in his writings, were proven to be untrue. Perhaps most intriguingly, Bielek claimed to have no memories of the Philadelphia Experiment until he saw the movie in 1984, a detail that raises eyebrows given the striking similarity between his story and the film. His struggles with paranoia and psychological issues, coupled with his financial reliance on selling CDs and merchandise at UFO conventions, culminated in his death in 2007. Despite discrepancies, some continue to believe his story, asserting that a government-sponsored disinformation campaign aimed to discredit him.

The focus then shifts to Stewart Swerdlow, another prominent figure claiming to be a Montauk Boy. Swerdlow's assertions stretch beyond the project, encompassing extraordinary claims such as speaking ten unheard-of languages, having his DNA spliced with aliens, imprisonment by the Illuminati, and possessing abilities like seeing auric fields and traveling through hyperspace. His narrative touches on numerous conspiracy theories, from moon bases to lizard people. However, skepticism arises, especially given a judge's declaration that Swerdlow was a fraud. Despite his controversial reputation, Swerdlow offers deprogramming services for a fee and markets an array of products, including potions, vitamins, and even dog treats. The narrative raises caution against investing in his products, emphasizing the need for critical scrutiny when encountering such figures in the conspiracy realm.

The spotlight shifts to Preston Nichols, the central figure in the prevailing theory. Nichols himself acknowledges the dual nature of his narrative, presenting it as non-fiction without falsehoods while recognizing its potential interpretation as pure science fiction. However, doubts emerge as inconsistencies surface. Nichols claims the Montauk Experiment occurred deep underground, connected by tunnels to other secret locations in the United States. Yet, geological considerations challenge this assertion. Long Island, including Montauk, is predominantly composed of glacial moraine—debris left by receding glaciers. This sandy terrain limits deep excavation, a fact evident in the absence of skyscrapers beyond downtown Manhattan, where bedrock allows for substantial digging.

A disconcerting revelation surfaces about Preston Nichols, the central figure in the Montauk Project theory. Nichols, known for his role in deprogramming individuals involved in the alleged experiments, is described to have employed a controversial technique. This method requires Nichols to touch individuals while they are in an aroused state, a detail withheld for sensitivity.

Nichols's deprogramming sessions involved a replica of the Montauk chair and a research room. Eyewitnesses reported that Nichols would enter the room with a young man, typically in his early 20s. After approximately 20 or 30 minutes, the individual would emerge disheveled, often appearing uneasy, while

Nichols himself would be covered in sweat. It is mentioned that Nichols deprogrammed as many as 25 Montauk boys, referred to as "disciples," a few times a week. These individuals shared a house near Nichols. The exact number of participants and sessions remains uncertain.

While the books depicting the Montauk Project present Nichols as a hero caught in an overwhelming conspiracy, the narrative challenges this portrayal. It asserts that, in truth, Preston Nichols can be viewed as a villain due to his involvement in the controversial deprogramming sessions and the proliferation of the Montauk Project theory. This revelation adds a dark layer to the narrative, complicating the perception of the central figure in this alleged conspiracy.

The Montauk House of Cards

Exposing Preston Nichols as a villain rather than the hero depicted in the Montauk Project theory. It emphasizes that Nichols, along with other individuals suffering from mental illness, addiction, or abuse, were exploited in the proliferation of the conspiracy theory.

The delusion of being part of the Montauk Project provided meaning to the lives of many individuals, offering them a sense of belonging and a new family united by shared experiences of pain. Preston Nichols, through deprogramming sessions, took advantage of these vulnerable young men for an extended period. Other dishonest individuals aided Nichols in constructing a complex narrative, one that continues to captivate followers.

The Montauk Project theory is acknowledged as having roots in factual government actions, such as drugging people against their will, kidnapping, and torture. However, it asserts that Nichols, Al Bielek, and Stuart Swerdlow introduced embellishments like time travel, aliens, and monster conjuring, forming a fragile house of cards. The interconnectedness of their stories is highlighted, emphasizing that if even one detail is debunked, the entire fraudulent narrative collapses.

◆ ◆ ◆

EPILOGUE

A Journey Beyond Time

As the final chapter unfolds, the pages of the time travel book turn, closing a narrative that transcends the boundaries of the imaginable. The exploration of temporal landscapes, paradoxes, and the very fabric of existence leaves readers with a lingering sense of wonder and contemplation.

A Tapestry of Possibilities:

The book, a chronicle of temporal escapades, weaves a tapestry of possibilities that stretch the limits of human comprehension. Each chapter, laden with the weight of speculative science and creative conjecture, invites readers to explore the vast expanse of the unknown.

Temporal Divergence:

The concept of multiple timelines and divergent realities unfolds like a flower, revealing intricate petals of what-ifs and alternate destinies. The notion that every decision, every moment, births a new universe sparks contemplation on the fragility and resilience of the temporal continuum.

Chronicles of the Unseen:

Within the pages, narratives unfold where time is both a benevolent guide and a relentless adversary. Characters traverse centuries, facing the consequences of their actions across epochs. The unseen hands of destiny manipulate the threads of time, leaving an indelible mark on the landscapes of the past, present, and future.

Temporal Ethics:

As readers journey through the time travel odyssey, ethical dilemmas surface like ripples on a temporal pond. The consequences of altering the past, the responsibility of holding the future in one's hands, and the delicate dance between fate and free will become threads woven into the fabric of the narrative.

The Echo of Possibility:

In the wake of the final chapter, the echo of possibility reverberates. The concept that time travel, though a product of imagination, carries the weight of philosophical inquiry challenges readers to question their perceptions of reality and the malleability of time itself.

A Timeless Reflection:

The epilogue invites readers to reflect on the timeless allure of time travel—a concept that transcends literary boundaries and resonates across cultures and epochs. The book's pages may close, but the exploration of temporal frontiers remains an ongoing journey in the collective human imagination.

As the last words fade, the book leaves readers with a tantalizing thought: What if, beyond the final page, the adventure continues in the uncharted territories of the temporal unknown? The journey, it seems, is never truly over.

ABOUT THE AUTHOR

Prabal Jain

Prabal Jain is a distinguished author and financial expert, renowned for his insightful contributions to the world of finance and investment. With a background as a Chartered Accountant and a successful career in finance, Prabal brings a wealth of knowledge and expertise to his writing.

We publish Business books that are concise, straightforward and take no longer than one hour to read.

Receive our new eBooks for free.

Sign up at: www.read.riverwoodcapital.me

BOOKS BY THIS AUTHOR

Mossad's Top-Secret Missions Exposed: Secrets Of Israel's Elite Intelligence Agency

Dive into the world of Mossad, Israel's renowned intelligence agency, and unravel the secrets behind their top-secret missions in this riveting book. From high-stakes covert operations to diplomatic negotiations, this meticulously researched account offers a deep insight into Mossad's history and its crucial role in shaping Israel's destiny. Discover the hidden stories of espionage, political maneuvering, and the challenges faced by Mossad agents as they navigate the tumultuous Middle East. A must-read for anyone intrigued by the world of intelligence and the geopolitics of the region, this book delivers a comprehensive look at Mossad's actions, successes, and setbacks up to the year 2020. Uncover the covert world of Mossad and its impact on global events as you journey through this remarkable book.

Starbucks: A Coffee Empire's Rise And Roast: From Beans To Billions: Decoding Starbucks' Global Triumph

Embark on a captivating journey through the aromatic realms of Starbucks with "Starbucks: A Coffee Empire's Rise and Roast." This enthralling narrative takes you from the modest beginnings of Starbucks in 1971 to its status as a global coffee empire with a staggering $22 billion valuation.

Manufactured by Amazon.ca
Acheson, AB